The
MULBERRY
TREE

The
MULBERRY
TREE

Allison Rushby

CANDLEWICK PRESS

Copyright © 2018 by Allison Rushby

First U.S. edition 2020
First published by Walker Books (Australia) 2018

Library of Congress Catalog Card Number pending
ISBN 978-1-5362-0761-3

20 21 22 23 24 25 LBM 10 9 8 7 6 5 4 3 2 1

Printed in Melrose Park, IL, U.S.A.

This book was typeset in Centaur.

Candlewick Press
99 Dover Street
Somerville, Massachusetts 02144

visit us at www.candlewick.com

To the villages of Buckden,
Offord D'Arcy, Offord Cluny,
Hemingford Grey, and Hemingford Abbots
for the year of inspiration and to
Gabi James for her warm welcome

Do naught wrong by the mulberry tree,
or she'll take your daughters . . .

one,

two,

three.

In the dead of night, spirited away,
never to see an eleventh birthday.

I

Into the Countryside

Immy sat in between her parents and watched as the woman in the dark blue suit stacked a pile of folders on her desk.

"You'll love Hemingford D'Arcy," the woman said. "I think you're making a very wise decision choosing village life. I mean, it would be equally amazing to live here, in the heart of Cambridge, but village life is so lovely. All that space, the thatched cottages, and the tiny village school. . . . There's a reason so many families move out of London and commute into the city for work, you know."

Immy, her mother, and her father blinked their dry, tired eyes and said nothing. The truth was, they *didn't* know. They'd come all the way from Sydney so that Immy's mother could work in a special hospital just outside Cambridge. None of them had even visited this city before. That's why her parents had hired this relocation woman—to help them find the right house and the right school. All three family members were sleepy and cranky. All they could think about was that it was midnight back at home and they'd rather be tucked into bed. Immy couldn't even remember what day it was. Wednesday? No, Thursday.

"Right." The woman stood, clutching her folders to her. One of them had a label on it that said HELEN, and Immy remembered this was the woman's name. Helen smiled at them brightly. "I can see you're exhausted. So let's get you on the road and find you somewhere to live, shall we? We've four properties to see today, and I'm sure one of them will be just what you're looking for." Glancing down at her desk, her eyes fell on a folder that still lay there. "Ah, that was what I meant to double-check. How old are you now, Imogen?"

"Almost eleven," Immy answered.

"But not eleven yet?"

"No, not yet. In about a month's time."

"I see." Helen smiled again, but Immy thought it looked forced now. She patted the folder that remained on her desk and left it where it was. "Let's go, shall we?"

Helen's black Mercedes whizzed around the lush green countryside as she showed Immy and her parents rental properties. After they'd visited two houses, Immy began to feel as if they might be acting out a strange version of "Goldilocks and the Three Bears." Everything was too big, too small, too hot, too cold, except that in their version of the story, nothing, unfortunately, was just right. The first house was too dark and poky and smelled like mold. The second house—a converted barn—looked good from the outside, but when they got inside, it was obvious that something had gone very wrong with the decorating. Everything was too modern, with blue lights, ultra-white tiles, and a stainless-steel kitchen.

"It reminds me of being in theater." Immy's mum, a heart surgeon, had stared around in horror.

"It reminds me of *Star Trek*," her dad had said. He'd

walked over to stand behind the kitchen bench and spread his arms wide along the countertop, a serious expression falling over his face. "Captain's log, stardate 2386.8. We have not yet located the house we are seeking. We will therefore continue our journey into the unknown Cambridgeshire countryside."

Immy had laughed, though she wasn't entirely sure why — whether at her father's joke or at him thinking he was captain of this trip. It hadn't been her dad who had shuffled them off to the other side of the world after things had gone terribly wrong.

Next up had been a very tidy, very neat little brick house in a row of very tidy, very neat little brick houses. Immy's mother had been dubious because of its lack of character.

"Do you think the Dursleys live on the left- or the right-hand side?" she'd whispered to Immy when Helen was out of earshot.

So that one was a no as well. Helen hadn't seemed all that upset. She'd herded the Watts family outside, the sky beginning to turn gray above. When Helen had started up the car once more, she'd taken a moment to turn around and look at Immy and her dad in the back seat.

"I've saved the best till last. I think you'll love the next place. It's a very pretty three-bedroom apartment in a converted mill. It's next to a lock — you know, like a water elevator for boats — so you'd be able to watch the canal boats coming and going all summer long. There's a swan, and she has eight fluffy gray cygnets right now. *And* it's less than a mile's walk through the woods to school. It's rather idyllic, actually."

"It sounds lovely," Immy's mum had replied, sounding hopeful.

And it was. The old mill itself was amazing — a big, cookie-colored brick building. It squatted next to an old, skinny stone bridge that could take only one car at a time. The river flowed briskly underneath, and, as promised, the white swan and her fluffy gray cygnets swam leisurely up and down, completing the picture.

But again, it wasn't quite right. Good, but not quite right.

"I'm not sure.... We've never lived in an apartment before. I'd really hoped for our own garden," Immy's mum said as they walked back to the car, the gravel crunching under their feet.

"The complex does have a private flower meadow."

Helen gestured to a small wooden gate that led to a field beyond.

"Can't say I've ever had my own flower meadow before," Immy's dad said.

"They're hard to come by in inner-city Sydney," her mum replied. She sighed and turned back to Helen. "If we've seen all the suitable properties you have, we'll take tonight to think about this one. I suppose we knew we'd have to compromise on something. It might simply have to be the garden."

A sudden gust of wind sent their hair and coats whipping around them, and the foursome made their way quickly toward the car.

Helen navigated the thin stone bridge that led from the converted mill back to the village, and soon enough, they turned right onto the village's long main street with its quaint thatched cottages. Painted pink, yellow, white, and terra-cotta, they were so pretty they didn't look quite real, but rather more like something from an old-fashioned Christmas card. From the back seat, Immy kept a close watch on her mother, who looked out the car window wistfully. This is what she'd really wanted. Immy had seen her mother looking night after night at the real estate sites on the internet. She wanted a perfect thatched cottage with a perfect garden to try to make them a perfect life in—to make things better again. Immy glanced over at her father, who noticed her stare and quickly rearranged his expression to something approximating a smile. He did that a lot lately. Immy hated it. Scowling, she turned to her window once more.

Which is when she saw it.

"Stop!" she said, reaching out and thumping the back of Helen's seat. "STOP!"

2

Lavender Cottage

Helen pulled the car over immediately and hit the curb with a bump. "What? What is it?" she said. "Are you feeling carsick?"

Immy didn't answer her. She'd already unbuckled her seat belt and opened the car door, and she was getting out. Her eyes were fixed upon a house of creamy white with the prettiest canary-yellow door. Thatch coated the roof like a thick icing and the cherry on top was a straw pigeon, who seemed to strut around on the roof as if he owned the place. The garden heaved with lavender that spilled out over the white wooden fence. Immy ran her hand along it and then sniffed her fingers, inhaling the bright scent. But what had really caught her eye sat right by the gate itself—a sign that read FOR LEASE. The exact same yellow-and-blue sign that had been on all the houses they'd visited today.

By now, Immy's mum had exited the car and was standing beside her. Her dad appeared on her other side only seconds later.

It took Helen a moment or two longer to reach them. She said nothing, her jaw set in a hard line.

"This looks ideal," Immy's mum said. "Can we see it?"

"Ah . . ." was Helen's only answer.

Immy looked up to see disappointment written all over her mother's face. "Oh, is it rented already?"

"I . . ."

Now Immy and her parents stared at Helen.

Finally, Helen shook her head. "I'm sorry, but this isn't the property for you."

Immy's mum frowned, confused. "Why ever not?" she said. "It seems to tick so many of our boxes. It's a character house. It's close to the school. It has a beautiful garden. Is it out of our price range?"

"No." Helen looked up and down the street like she was checking to see if anyone was watching them. "It's not about money."

"Then we'd like to see it, please." Immy's mum's voice was firm. It was obvious that she was getting crankier by the minute. If Helen knew what was good for her, she'd open up the house immediately.

Maybe Helen sensed this, because she headed back toward the car. "I left the folder with all the information back at the office." She paused here as if she hoped Immy's mum would change her mind. Immy remembered the folder that Helen had left on her desk.

"That's all right," Immy's mum said firmly. "We'd still like to view it. Do you have the keys?"

Helen's shoulders sagged. "Yes," she answered, going over to open the trunk of the car. She fished around in a large metal box and pulled out some keys.

The foursome approached the wooden gate that opened and shut with a friendly creak, the scent of the lavender enveloping them as they took the few steps to the front door. Among the bushes, large bumblebees buzzed busily, and wildflowers swayed here and there in the breeze, as if dancing to an unheard tune. By the door itself, a little hand-painted ceramic plaque read LAVENDER COTTAGE. Helen opened the front door.

"Oh!" Immy's mum said, the first one through the door. "It's full of furniture. There's still someone living here."

"No," Helen replied. "The family is renting it furnished."

Following her father, Immy stepped forward to get a better look inside, and her eyes widened. She'd never seen anything like it. It was almost like being in a doll's house. The minuscule slate-tiled entryway led directly into the living area. This was tiny—only big enough for a warm yellow sofa and two large matching armchairs in the same fabric, which faced the large brick fireplace. The walls were painted the same creamy white as the outside of the house, and, on all sides, heavy black wooden beams hugged the room tightly.

Immy's dad stepped into the living room itself. "Well?" He looked up at the low ceiling and then back at Immy. "Am I going to make it?"

Immy watched as his head cleared a beam. "Just!"

"Maybe it's a sign." He waggled his eyebrows at her.

But Immy's mum wasn't interested in any of this, her gaze focused hard on Helen. "The family is renting it furnished? But we *specifically* asked to look at furnished properties. I simply don't understand why you didn't show us this property first."

"I . . . because . . ." Helen stammered.

But Immy didn't wait to listen to Helen's explanation. Her attention was fixed on the room behind them. She had the strangest feeling. Like she simply *had* to go in there. She passed by the three adults, crossed the entryway, and made her way through into the tiny dining room. It consisted mostly of a cupboard and a small, round wooden table with four chairs. The feeling that she had to keep going became stronger still. So much so that it made her feel light-headed. She continued through into the kitchen, which had pale wooden cabinets polished to a high sheen. The walls were painted a fresh, welcoming green, and, again, the black wooden beams felt heavy overhead.

Outside.

Another wave swept over her, and Immy spun on her heel. That was what she wanted—to go outside.

Her eyes locked onto the other side of the dining area, where French doors led out to what must be the garden. Immy walked over to them as if in a trance.

Her hand was already on the metal handle when she heard high heels clattering across the gray slate floor.

"No!" Helen's voice called out. "Imogen! Stop!"

Immy jolted and turned to look at Helen just as her parents appeared behind the agent, questioning looks on both their faces.

She realized the feeling had gone. She felt normal again.

Helen's hand flew to her chest, as if relieved to see that Immy was still inside. "You can't go out there. You're a girl, and you're almost eleven. It's simply not safe."

3

The Mulberry Tree

Silence fell over the small room.

"I'm sorry, did I just hear you correctly?" Immy's dad finally spoke. He and Immy's mother entered the room and came to stand on either side of their daughter.

Helen leaned against the door frame. "Yes, you heard me correctly." She looked weary as she held up a hand. "You're going to think what I'm about to say is ridiculous. Trust me, I don't usually believe in things like this. Not at all. The truth is, people . . . well, they wouldn't like it if they knew I'd brought your daughter here. The family who owns the house is still in the village, but they didn't want to live here for the next few years, because they have a girl themselves. They've rented a furnished house a few streets away. Here, I'll show you what I'm talking about, but please don't go outside."

Helen made her way across the room and squeezed by Immy and her parents.

She opened the French doors wide.

Immy and her parents crowded around to look at what on earth could be outside. Immy honestly had no idea. A sinkhole? Maybe even a *wormhole*, the way Helen was carrying on.

They were met with a view of a large garden, but unlike in the welcoming front of the house, no flowers bloomed and no bumblebees buzzed. Everything was dark and drenched in shadow because of what stood to the left——a gigantic tree that loomed over the entire garden and the house itself. Immy's breath caught in her throat, and her heart began to race as her eyes slowly traveled up its thick, gnarled trunk. Halfway up, armlike branches began to shoot out threateningly, dividing into stout black fingers that poked and taunted the house cruelly. It was summer, yet the tree displayed no green. Not one leaf. Just inky blackness that blocked out the sky above. It was almost as if the tree were attempting to swallow the cottage whole.

It was hideous. The most hideous, ugly, nasty-looking, bad-tempered tree that Immy had ever seen.

She couldn't take her eyes off it.

"What a mulberry it is," Immy's dad said. "It must be ancient."

"It is," Helen said. "At least five hundred years old, though the cottage itself dates from the seventeenth century."

"I'm surprised it's lasted as long as it has," Immy's mother said. "It's awful."

Maybe it was Immy's imagination, but as soon as the words exited her mother's mouth, she felt as if the tree's fingers reached out farther. Closing in on the house. On *her*. Taking a step backward, she bumped into her dad.

"Don't say that," Helen said sharply.

"Well, I don't think it can hear me." Immy's mum gave Helen a look.

"Can it?" Immy asked, the words coming before she could stop them. Up until now, she hadn't believed trees could hear, but this one . . . she wasn't so sure.

Helen's eyes met hers. "There are lots of people in

the village who think it can—who believe the tree's bewitched. The thing is, over the years, there have been two girls who've . . . well . . . simply disappeared from this house on the eve of their eleventh birthdays. That's why I asked you about your own birthday."

Immy, her mum, and her dad all stared at Helen with open mouths.

"Are you serious?" Immy's dad said.

But they could all see that she was.

"It sounds to me like you've got a shady character in the village rather than a tree. I take it this was all investigated by the police?" Immy's mum said.

"There wasn't a formal police force here until the mid–1800s or so, and the first girl was before then—in the late 1700s, I think. The second case must have been investigated, because she went missing in 1945, but as far as I know they never found out what happened to her. Do you see the two large knots in the trunk of the tree?"

Immy and her parents all inspected the trunk as best as they could from afar. Just as Helen had said, there were two large knots that were visible—one higher up on the tree's trunk and one lower down. Immy could see that there was some sort of flower lying directly below the bottom knot. It looked like a small white rose, which seemed strange, because there were no flowers in the garden.

"They say a new knot appeared after each girl went missing—that the tree somehow captured their souls."

In the shadow of the tree, Immy shivered.

"This is why the owners have moved out for a while. Their daughter's eleventh birthday is coming up."

"Honestly, that's the silliest thing I've ever heard. What superstitious nonsense!" Immy's mum said, breaking the eerie mood. "Knots in trees are formed by all sorts of natural things—dead branches, pruning, disease. They've got nothing at all to do with little girls disappearing."

Immy had to agree with her mother—it *was* the silliest, most superstitious thing she'd ever heard as well. And yet, as she stood there in the presence of the mulberry tree . . .

She believed every word of it.

Helen simply shrugged.

"If they feel so strongly about the tree, why hasn't someone gotten rid of it?" Immy's father asked.

"Because of its age, it has a protection order," Helen told him. "They can't."

"Any fruit?" he asked.

Helen gave him a withering look. "Apparently it used to produce bucketfuls, but it stopped when the first girl disappeared."

Immy's mum made a noise that was somewhere between a snort and a laugh. "Well, I'm going to look at the rest of the house," she said. "Coming, Immy?"

Immy took one last look at the tree. "All right," she said after a moment or two. She followed her mother into the kitchen, where she spent a lot of time going on about some kind of stove called an Aga. From here they crossed back to the entryway and went up the narrow stairs, Immy running her hands over the beams on the wall as she went. Upstairs, she realized the house consisted of only four real rooms. Downstairs were the living room and the dining room/kitchen, and upstairs were a large bedroom and a smaller bedroom, with a tiny bathroom sandwiched in between. Immy turned right, into the small bedroom. The spaces in between the black beams were painted a welcoming lemon-yellow, and a slim mirrored wardrobe reflected the color, making the room look larger than it was. There was an old but freshly painted white desk and chair and a white chest of drawers. A single white iron bed frame was pushed up against the right-hand wall.

Immy crossed the room and approached the window, hesitating with her last step. Just as she'd suspected, there was the mulberry tree, its cronelike fingers tapping rhythmically upon the window itself. She jumped as a creak came from outside the door to the room.

"I hope I didn't scare you downstairs," Helen said, a worried look on her face.

"No," Immy replied, though the truth was, her heart was thumping away inside her chest. "It's all right."

Both of Immy's parents appeared behind Helen, and they all squished into the room. Just as Immy had done herself, her dad crossed over to the window and peered out at the tree once more.

"I know the house itself is charming, but to be honest, I'm not sure the owners would even consider your application," Helen told them.

Immy's gaze moved immediately to her mother's face. Uh-oh. It wasn't wise to tell her mother she couldn't do something. However, Immy was surprised to see that her mother didn't really look all that convinced about the cottage. She came over to stand behind Immy and hugged her to her side.

"Let's head back to Cambridge," she said to Helen. "We'll give you a call as soon as we've decided what to do."

4
A Decision

After sneaking in a nap, Immy's mum went off to the hospital to get her ID card. Immy and her dad went exploring, taking a punting tour on the River Cam — a ride in which a student pushed their thin, flat-bottomed boat with a long pole. They sat on fat cushions and slipped silently and smoothly under the low arches of stone bridges. They spied on the grassy backs of the colleges, Immy running her hand in the cool water when her father wasn't looking.

The family met up for dinner at a pizza place. Immy's dad wrote down on a paper napkin a list of the houses they'd visited.

"So." His pen hovered. "Which one are we crossing off first?"

"The moldy one," Immy and her mother said at exactly the same time.

He crossed it off.

The Dursley house was struck next. Then the *Star Trek* house.

Which left only the apartment in the converted mill and Lavender Cottage.

Immy's dad frowned as he stared at the napkin. "I can't believe they named it that," he said. "Surely something else would be more appropriate. Like Killer Tree Cottage, for example. Or maybe they shouldn't have called it anything at all and instead put up a BEWARE OF THE TREE sign?"

Both Immy and her mum laughed.

"So," he continued, "which is it to be?"

The threesome looked at one another.

Immy thought about the apartment. It was pretty, and the cygnets were sweet. It would be fun to feed them and walk to school through the woods every day and see the seasons change. But Lavender Cottage . . . Lavender Cottage was exciting. She shifted to thinking about the tree then, about its skinny fingers tip-tapping at the bedroom window. A shiver went up her spine.

"Lavender Cottage," she said quickly, before she could change her mind.

"Really?" her parents both said, staring at her. They looked surprised.

"You're not worried about the evil tree?" her mum asked.

Of course she was. But the thing was—as much as she wanted to run away from the tree, she was also drawn to it, desperate to know more.

"You said this would be an adventure," Immy said to her mum. "And here it is."

"When I said this would be an adventure, I didn't exactly mean I wanted to put you in danger of being abducted."

Immy could see that her parents wanted her to take the easy option of the apartment. She'd have to convince them. She looked down at the table for a moment and thought before meeting her mother's gaze again. "A tree can't make a girl disappear," she said. "We all know that."

"Yes, but other things can," her dad replied quickly. "People can."

Immy took another second or two, working out the dates in her head. "We don't know anything about the first girl, but if someone took the second girl in 1945, well, they'd either be dead already or very, very old, wouldn't they? Anyway, I know all the rules. Don't talk to strangers. Don't get in other people's cars unless you've told me it's okay. And Dad will be home before and after school. He can even walk me to and pick me up from the school gate if he wants. Plus, my birthday's on a weekend. We could go away the night before if we really wanted to be sure."

Her parents looked at each other, and Immy knew from their expressions that she'd succeeded. Both doctors, they were very logical. There was nothing they enjoyed more than hearing a solid argument come out of her mouth.

"What do you think?" Immy's dad asked her mum. "Should we really go for it?"

For the next few minutes, Immy's parents discussed the pros and cons of putting in an application on the cottage while Immy watched her father. He was caught up in the discussion, and for that brief, shiny moment, Immy thought his eyes looked like his old eyes—clear and not clouded with thoughts of the past.

In the end, her mother insisted they sleep on it and make a final decision in the morning. Just in case anyone changed their mind.

5

Whispers in the Night

There were whispers in the night. In Immy's dreams, words curled around the tree's limbs, which felt for her in the dark. Girls danced around the trunk, singing a strange song she didn't know. She woke briefly with a start as other voices — real voices — hushed each other, and she fell back to sleep.

The bang of the hotel room door wrenched her from sleep yet again, and Immy lifted her head to see that it was light. Her dad entered, carrying a tray of hot drinks, a paper bag held between his teeth. She could smell cinnamon and butter.

"Sorry, sweetheart," he said when he'd put the paper bag down on the small table in the room.

"I didn't mean to wake you. Raisin toast? Hot chocolate?"

Immy yawned and nodded at the same time. She was about to ask where her mother was, but then she realized she could hear the shower running. She clambered up from her rollaway bed and went over to sit down with her father at the table. He placed her hot chocolate in front of her, carefully lifted the lid, and then split open the greasy brown paper bag containing the toast. Immy took a piece and tried not to look as her father popped two pills out of their silver-shelled homes. He took them both at once with a swig of water, leaving the packet shining in the sunlight on the table. As Immy watched him, she remembered the whispers from last night. There'd been whispers about those pills as well over the last month. Her father hadn't wanted to take them. It was all right for him to feel sad, he'd argued to Immy's mum.

Her mum hadn't agreed. And now he took the two pills once a day.

Immy glanced out the window next to her and watched the people hurrying over the cobbled street below, juggling their handbags and briefcases, phones and coffees. She thought back farther then—to another night when she'd heard whispers. She'd been sleeping on a different rollaway bed—a trundle bed at her friend Grace's house. Just like last night, the voices had woken her. They'd become louder, clashing like steel swords.

Grace's father had moved out not long after.

Back then, Immy had thought something like that could never happen to her family. She couldn't have imagined nightly arguments and whispers and long, loaded silences. Her parents had always fought about things—about directions in the car, about expensive silk shirts that shouldn't have been washed with jeans, about who had used up the milk and not bought more. But not about things that really mattered. Not until this. Immy's chest felt suddenly tight. She glanced over at her father, who was reading the newspaper.

"How's the hot chocolate?" he asked without looking up.

"Good," Immy answered, even though she hadn't touched it yet.

Back in Australia, her dad had been a GP. He had worked in a practice with four other doctors in a big old wooden house in a suburb where there were lots of big old wooden houses. Many of the people who lived in those houses were also old, and lots of them were his patients. Every year, they would have to get her dad to sign a special certificate saying they were allowed to keep on driving. And every year, her dad had to tell some of his patients he couldn't sign the form, and their license would be taken away. He hated doing this, yet he knew that he had to — it just wasn't safe for them to drive anymore. He hadn't been surprised when he'd had to tell an eighty-three-year-old patient, Bob, that he couldn't sign his form that year. He'd barely been able to sign it the year before, and, over the twelve months that had passed, Bob's eyesight had gotten worse. Bob had begged him to sign the form. He'd reminded Immy's dad that he needed to travel the distance of a few suburbs each day to see his wife, who was in a nursing home. Her dad had suggested he could catch the bus, or perhaps his son could look into the taxi-subsidy offers that might be available to him. Her dad had checked Bob's chart, seen his son's phone number was on there, and made a note to himself to call the son later on if he had time. Unfortunately, Bob hadn't been able to take no for an answer. He'd pleaded, said he couldn't get by without his license. But her dad still wouldn't sign the form.

"I'm sorry," he'd told Bob. "It wouldn't be right."

Bob had stormed off, saying he'd find another doctor who'd sign the form.

Bob hadn't done this.

Instead, he'd kept driving his car. And six weeks later, he'd driven through a pedestrian crossing and killed a mother and her baby girl in her stroller.

As she remembered, Immy's hands clenched around her cup of hot chocolate, almost making it spill over the top.

No one had blamed her dad, but he had blamed himself.

If only he'd called the son. If only he'd spent a few more minutes with Bob, checking the bus route, showing him how it wouldn't be difficult to get to the nursing home. If only he'd looked into the taxi subsidy himself.

Months passed by, and Immy's father had spiraled ever downward into a bleak, black place lined with "if onlys." He couldn't sleep. He couldn't work.

And he couldn't seem to make Immy's mum understand why.

"I know you care," she'd tell him, over and over again. "It's what makes you such a wonderful GP. But you're not their babysitter. Their lives are theirs to live. You did the right thing by society in taking his license away. He knew full well he shouldn't have driven a car, and he did it anyway."

"It would have taken only a few minutes to care a bit more."

"All those minutes add up, Andrew. You had other patients to see. Sick patients who needed you."

"But . . ."

Her father had as many *buts* as he had *if onlys.*

Immy had *if onlys* herself. If only her dad could forget about what had happened with Bob. Stupid Bob who'd driven his car when he knew he wasn't allowed. After the accident, his heart and eyesight had grown steadily worse, and he'd ended up in the same nursing home as his wife. He hadn't even gone to jail! He'd only gone to court and had been given something called a suspended sentence.

Unbelievably, her dad had visited him in the nursing home. When her dad had returned from seeing him, he'd told her that Bob had cried. Immy had been mad about this. In fact, she'd been furious.

She'd yelled at her dad. Screamed at him for going. She'd been surprised at how angry she'd been. It was as if all the feelings she'd been pushing down inside had bubbled up and gushed out at once. Her dad had sat her down and tried to explain why he'd gone. He'd told her that what she needed to understand was that everyone was fighting their own battles in life. Yes, Bob had made terrible choices—not because he was a bad person at heart, but because he'd been afraid and desperate to keep his wife happy. He hadn't wanted them to be separated after living their whole lives together. Immy had refused to see her dad's point. In her mind, Bob had gotten exactly what he'd wanted: now he lived with his wife and didn't need a car at all. Immy had said he should be locked up forever. Her dad had simply sighed and told her that Bob had made his own prison and he'd punish himself in it until the end of his days.

The bathroom door opened, and Immy's mum appeared.

"Ah, you're up!" she said, pointing her toothbrush at them both. "And having breakfast. Good work."

Immy waited to see if her dad would take this the wrong way. It happened a lot these days. Trying to keep the peace, she shoved half a piece of toast in her mouth before her dad realized she hadn't touched any of her food yet.

"So, we have a decision to make," her mother said. "I was thinking . . . if we're not sure about Lavender Cottage or the apartment in the converted mill, we could always look at places in Cambridge itself. It doesn't matter if we take a little longer."

Immy chewed and looked from her mum to her dad to see what he was going to say. It was good, she thought, this moving around, being busy. It kept everyone occupied. There wasn't so much time to think. She stopped chewing for a second as she realized something. What would happen when they stopped again? When they figured everything out and moved into a house or an apartment, she went to school, her mother went to work, and there was nothing left for her dad to do.

At that very moment, she looked back at her mum and noticed her eyes move to the silver pill packet on the table.

"Yes, I've taken them," her dad said flatly, noticing, too.

Staring at the pill packet, Immy realized that

maybe Lavender Cottage could be useful in another way. Having that tree around—it might take her parents' minds off everything else. Maybe if they could all keep worrying about the tree, there wouldn't be time to argue about other things, like pills. Or for her dad to remember why he was taking them in the first place. After last night's dream, Immy had wondered if the apartment might be the smarter choice, but the thought of everyone being happily preoccupied decided it.

"Ithinkweshouldtakeit." The words came out of Immy's mouth in a rush, as did a bit of raisin toast, unfortunately. "Sorry." She wiped it up with a napkin. "I mean, I think we should take the cottage. I think we should go and tell Helen right now that we want it. The cottage . . . it's everything we said we wanted, except for a silly old tree that people go on about." She didn't want to call the tree names, and her words came out too fast again, but she had to convince her parents somehow.

Her parents looked at each other silently for a moment or two. And then they both shrugged.

"You're sure?" her mother asked.

"Sure sure?" her dad checked.

No, Immy thought. But it was a different word that exited her mouth. "Yes." She stood, almost knocking her hot chocolate over in the process.

Her mother's mouth twisted. "I don't know. It might seem like a good idea now, but—"

"A tree isn't going to take me away in the night," Immy cut in. "It's just a made-up story."

Her parents' eyes met. Finally, her dad shrugged.

"Let's go and see Helen. Right now," Immy said.

Her dad gave her a once-over. "You might want to change out of your pajamas first."

"Good idea," Immy said, jumping over the rollaway bed and lunging for her suitcase.

The truth was, she would have quite happily made the trip in her pajamas if it meant her dad forgetting about Bob. Even if it was just for a little while.

6

A Place to Call Home

Luckily, Helen was at her desk when Immy, along with her mother and father, pushed open the heavy glass door of the real estate office.

"We've made our decision." Immy's mum got straight to the point, not even bothering to sit down. "We'd like to apply for a year's lease on Lavender Cottage."

Helen stood. "Ah." There was a short silence as she stared at the three of them. "Well, as you know, you've been preapproved by our company and your references checked and so on. It's simply a matter of my calling the owners to discuss. I did give them a quick ring last night, though they weren't sure because of your, er . . . situation." Her eyes came to rest on Immy.

Immy's parents said nothing.

Helen cleared her throat. "However, the cottage hasn't been rented for some time, so you might just get lucky."

The tension between the three adults was stifling. Immy began to think Helen would persuade the owners to rent the place just so she could get rid of Immy's family.

"Would you like to duck out for a coffee while I call them?"

"No," Immy's mum told her. "We'll wait."

Everyone glanced over at the tiny waiting area only yards to their left. It consisted of the tiniest of coffee tables and four hard wooden stools. It was more for decoration than for waiting.

"Of course." Helen smiled the fakest of smiles now. "I won't be a moment."

Immy and her parents moved over to the waiting area and sat down. They didn't pick up any of the magazines on the table, and neither of her parents got out their phone. Instead, everyone listened in as Helen called the owners of Lavender Cottage.

"Hello, Jessica. Yes, the family I spoke to you about last night have come back in. They'd like to rent the cottage for a year . . ." Her voice changed to a whisper. "Yes, as I said, I've told them everything. . . . Mmm. . . . Eleven in a month's time . . . I don't know, they don't seem to mind. . . ." There was a long pause, as the owner must have spoken at length. "Well, all right, then, if you're sure."

There was the clunk of a phone being put down, then the sound of an office chair being wheeled backward. Immy and her parents all stood as Helen approached, that fake smile plastered across her face again.

"If you'd like the cottage, it's yours for twelve months," she said. "As you know, it includes all the furniture, and the washing machine and fridge are built in, so all you'll need are the essentials. Our firm has a rental service that can supply linen, dishes and glassware, and so on, if you like. We could deliver by late this afternoon."

"That sounds perfect, Helen." Immy's mum smiled her own fake smile in return.

"I'll print the forms out now." Helen moved back to her desk, Immy's mum following in her wake.

Immy turned to her dad, who rubbed his hands together. "House sorted," he said. "Next stop, rent a car."

By midday, Immy and her parents had gotten their keys to the cottage, rented a car, checked out of their hotel, picked up a few groceries, and made their way to Lavender Cottage.

"Want to do the honors?" Her dad passed her the key to the glossy yellow front door. Immy stuck it in the lock, turned the knob, and opened the door wide.

Inside, all was quiet. The threesome moved into the small entryway and looked around. Immy closed her eyes for a moment, wondering if she'd feel that strange sensation she'd felt yesterday. The one that had drawn her toward the garden. If she'd hear anything.

But there was nothing.

If anything, it was a little bit *too* quiet.

It was her father who moved off first, going to sit in one of the easy chairs in the living room, facing the fireplace. He pushed his hands out in front of himself as if warming them.

"My own fireplace," he said. "I can't wait to get a roaring fire going in there."

Her mum laughed. "It's summer! You're such a caveman."

"Just imagine. Christmas, a fire, roasted chestnuts, some eggnog, the Christmas tree over there." He pointed to a corner of the room.

"You've got it all worked out," her mother said.

"Can I have a puppy?" Immy said.

Her parents both laughed. "Nice try," they said at the same time.

Watching them, Immy's heart skipped a beat as it remembered how things used to be.

But then her dad got up. "Dream's over, sunshine. Time to unpack your suitcase before the truck gets here."

Immy's dad lugged her suitcase up to her bedroom, unlocked it, and undid the zipper. "Have fun!" he told his daughter with a teasing grin.

Immy waited until he'd gone and slowly looked around the room, taking it all in — the desk, the chair, the chest of drawers, the bed, the mirrored wardrobe.

And, of course, the tree, casting its long shadow outside. The breeze must have picked up, because the very tip of a branch scraped against the window with a slow and steady screech, the noise making every single hair on Immy's arms stand on end.

When the icky feeling had subsided, she strode over to the window, averted her eyes, and drew the curtains. She tried to convince herself that she wasn't scared of the tree, that she just needed time to get used to it. To its presence. To its noises.

It was just a tree.

Screech. The noise came again.

"Oh, shush," she told it, sounding a whole lot braver than she felt. She turned her back to the window.

That done, she was able to concentrate on the room itself.

The truth was, unpacking *was* kind of fun. Once the boring bits like putting away toiletries and hanging up clothes had been done, working out where she'd put things like photos and her stationery was nice. She wondered about the girl whose room this had been before her. What was she like? What had the room looked like then? Would they be in the same class at school? Would they be friends?

"Immy!" her dad had finally called out after an hour or so had passed.

"Yep?"

"Sandwiches!"

It was only then that she realized how hungry she was. She abandoned the few books she'd brought with her and ran down the steep stairs. Rounding the corner, she was in the dining room/kitchen in an instant.

"Whoa. Slower on those stairs, please," her mum said as she ferried juices and sandwiches from the fridge to the dining room table.

"Okay." Immy's eyes were on her father, who was standing by the French doors, which were open.

"Do we dare?" He held his hand out toward her.

Immy crossed the room. And when she reached her father, she took his hand, even though she thought she was far too old to do so.

7

In the Garden

Immy stared at the ground until they were directly under the tree itself. She could hear her heartbeat in her ears. It was so loud she was sure the tree could hear it, too.

Another noise caught her attention. There, woven through the thumping of her heart. Something else. Something higher, almost floating. Like a song. She knew it from somewhere. Remembered it somehow.

The sound was lost as Immy's gaze moved up, the sky poisoned by the tree's branches. The tree smelled strange. Musty and old, like it was stuffed full of decaying secrets.

A flash of something bright caught her eye, and

she saw that another white rose was wedged into the bottom knot. Immy looked around to make sure, but there were definitely no white roses growing in the garden. In fact, there was nothing growing in the garden other than the hedges, some patchy grass, and, near the little wooden gate, one struggling tree that looked like it was trying to run away. It was then that she realized her father had dropped her hand and was over by the thick hedge itself. She ran over to him, not wanting to be alone next to the tree.

"The hedges need a good trim," he said, running a hand along them. "Helen said we could pay to get the gardening done, but apparently the family has left all the gardening tools in the shed. I thought I'd do it. Stretch my gardening muscles, you know." He moved over toward the wooden shed in the corner of the garden. "Ah, the benefits of country living. It's unlocked." He opened the door and took a look inside. "Mower, hedge trimmer . . . even an old wooden playpen. Think we can use it to keep you out of trouble?" He glanced back at her.

Immy gave him a look.

He closed the door, and they moved on to the very back of the garden.

"And what do we have here?" he said as they approached the wooden gate.

Her dad opened it and they passed through.

"Oh!" Immy said, seeing they were in someone else's garden now, which was full of green grass, immaculate hedges, and masses of beautiful white roses.

Realizing they were trespassing, they took a step back again and reclosed the gate behind them.

"Maybe we can borrow cups of sugar?" her dad said.

"Or gardening tips?" Immy suggested, glancing back at their patchy grass.

"Point taken."

Still in the mood to explore, they moved off past the shed again, skimming the hedges once more, and made their way down the side of the house to the front garden.

Here, an explosion of life met their eyes. The lavender stood to attention, blending purple with the red of the poppies. The fat bumblebees continued to drone lazily above the colorful surface like fish over coral. As she watched them, Immy realized she could hear singing. Up and down the voices went in a sort of schoolyard singsong. Like "Ring a Ring o' Roses" or "Lucy Locket."

That was it—the song she'd heard just before. And last night, too, in her dream. She whipped around, seeking the sound. Directly across the road was a man, watching them. She noticed three girls standing farther down the road, also looking on. But, strangely, they weren't singing.

No one was.

Maybe she'd just imagined the song?

Immy's gaze remained on the three girls. There were two fair ones and one with dark hair and dark eyes who stared at her curiously.

Immy's dad turned to see what she was looking at. "Those girls are about your age. Surely they'll be at school with you. Go on over and say hello!"

Immy wondered if he remembered being a kid.

"No," she said.

"I'll come with you if you like."

Obviously he didn't remember being a kid *at all.*

"Go on."

"No."

"Go on."

"No!"

"Go on!"

"You're not going to give up until I go over there, are you?"

"No." Her father stole her own answer, loving every minute of this.

But before they could continue their argument, the man on the other side of the road beckoned them over.

"Would you mind?" he called out.

Immy's dad looked down at her. "How about we both go?"

The pair let themselves out the front gate and made their way across the road.

"Sorry to drag you over here," the man said with a chuckle as they approached. "It's just I'm originally from the village myself. It's an old superstition that you should walk on this side of the road. Because of the tree."

There was a short silence.

"Really?" Immy's dad finally replied. "What a pity."

"What do you mean?" the man said.

"I mean it's a pity that no one walks in front of the house. It's got a beautiful garden."

The man laughed. "Yes, I suppose it does. Out the front, anyway." He stuck his hand out. "I'm Mark Godwin. From the *Hemingford D'Arcy News.*"

"Andrew Watts." Immy's dad shook his hand. "And this is my daughter, Imogen. The local newspaper, eh? We've got quite a pile of those at home next to the fireplace."

Immy shot her father a look. He liked to talk but sometimes didn't think very hard before he let the words come out.

Seeing Immy's expression, he finally realized what he'd said. "That is . . . I meant . . . I noticed them. I read a couple the other evening. Looks like a top-quality publication. I'm sure it'll be useful for working out what's going on in the area."

Mark nodded. "Well, there's not much that we miss. Word gets around fast here. When we heard someone was moving into Lavender Cottage, I thought I could write a piece." With this, he brought out a little notebook and a pen.

Immy's dad looked surprised. "On us? There's not much to know, really. My wife's a heart surgeon. She's over here for a year for a bit of specialist training. And I'm . . . taking a sabbatical."

"Right, right . . ." Mark jotted this down in his notebook, but Immy couldn't help noticing that his gaze kept moving over to her. "You'll be going to school here, Imogen?"

"Yes," Immy answered, glancing at the three girls, who she realized were edging their way toward the group, behind her father, who couldn't see them from his position.

"She's really looking forward to it," Immy's dad said.

"Of course! Er, how old are you, Imogen?"

Ugh. She knew that's what he was really after all along. Immy's mouth set into a fixed line.

"I see," Immy's dad answered for her. "So this is about the tree. I don't think we want any pieces written about that, thank you very much. It'll just spread more nonsense."

"Nonsense? So you don't believe in the curse?"

Immy's father frowned. "Well, we'd hardly move in if we did, would we?"

"I suppose not."

"It's ridiculous to think a tree can take a child. Take it where exactly?"

"Child*ren*," Mark replied.

Seeing what was coming, Immy's gaze shot over to the three girls who were now within earshot. "Dad . . ." she warned.

But it was too late.

"It doesn't matter how many! Look — and this is all off the record; I don't want you quoting me and blackening our name in the village — from what I understand, the first disappearance wasn't investigated at all. Anything could have happened. The later one was probably one of those bungled investigations. Goodness knows, it's not like the police had access to decent technology, *and* there was a war going on. Not to mention that thing about the knots in the tree. Honestly, it's just as my wife was telling the real estate agent. Any simpleton knows knots on trees are caused by branches dying or pruning or disease. Not by abducted children. Lavender Cottage is a beautiful house with a beautiful garden and a very old mulberry tree, and that's it. The family is mad to have moved out of it. It's their poor daughter I feel sorry for. I mean, imagine letting your child grow up thinking a tree was going to steal her away. Her parents must be crazy! But never fear, on the evening of Immy's birthday, we'll surround ourselves in a sea of four-leaf clovers and rabbits' feet and other superstitious knickknacks. You know, just in case the crazies are right." He finished his long-winded speech with a bark of a laugh.

Except nobody else laughed with him.

Immy stared up at her father in horror. She knew superstitious talk was one of his pet peeves, but did he have to go off about it here? Now? That was the thing with her dad. When it came to all things scientific, he could never quite believe that other people might not have the same views as him. He couldn't understand that people in the village actually believed the tree had taken those girls.

"Dad," she hissed. Caught up in his ranting, he still wasn't aware the three girls were standing behind him. But Immy knew. And as her dad had said exactly what he thought, Immy had been watching the girl with the dark hair closely. Watching as her face turned as thunderously dark as her hair. Now, without a word, the girl turned and stalked off, the other two girls following close behind.

Her dad turned then, frowning as he saw the girls. "Oh, dear," he said, realizing they'd heard everything.

Immy couldn't find the words to reply, but Mark's face scrunched up. "'Oh, dear, is about right. The girl with the dark hair? That was the other family's 'poor daughter.'"

8

The Village Green

The reporter, realizing he wasn't going to get anything out of Immy's dad that he could print, went on his way. Immy and her dad stood in silence for a while, digesting what had happened.

"The girls went that way," Immy's dad said eventually, pointing down the street. "I suppose I should go and apologize." He started off.

"But ... our sandwiches," Immy said, thinking that wasn't a very good idea. "Mum made sandwiches."

"They'll wait." He sighed. "Come on."

Immy knew he'd made up his mind. She could argue with him or she could follow him. She trudged behind him, hoping the girls had run home.

* * *

At the end of the street, they turned a sharp right and were immediately met with the sight of a large expanse of very green grass. It looked like a park.

"Ah, the village green," her dad said.

"The what?"

"It's like a big park. A meeting spot for the whole community. They probably have fetes here, bonfire nights, witch burnings, things like that."

"Witch burnings?" Immy raised an eyebrow.

"Well, nothing gets the community together like a good witch burning."

"Good thing you're not a witch, then," Immy said. Either way, she was pretty sure he'd soon be on the village's burn list. Crossing her arms, Immy inspected the place. There was a playground. Two, actually. A fenced-in one for smaller kids, with baby swings and a slide, and one for the bigger kids, with a huge wooden fort, a zip line, and some larger swings. Unfortunately, the three girls hadn't run home but had made their way here and were now hanging around at the bottom of the wooden fort. There were also some boys of around the same age sitting high up on the roof of the fort itself, where they shouldn't have been.

"Oh, great," Immy mumbled. Not only were the girls here, but so were the cool kids.

"I guess I should go over and apologize," Immy's dad said, taking a step forward.

Immy grabbed his arm. "No!"

"What?"

"You've made things bad enough. Don't make it any worse. *I'll* apologize."

"I don't think . . ."

"Do you want me to survive past day one at this school?" She glanced over at the girls again. They were huddled together, pointedly not looking at her while sneaking glances at her at the same time. "Try not to make it worse," she said as she began across the grass.

As she went, the girls stopped talking and turned to face her. Maybe sensing trouble was coming, the boys inched over to the edge of the fort to get a better view of the scene below. They seemed to be stuffing their faces with something. Something of a deep red that they were eating out of an upturned cap, of all things. It took her a few moments to realize they'd collected some berries from somewhere nearby.

"Hi," Immy said, reaching the three girls. The girl with the dark hair and deep brown eyes stood half a step in front of the other two girls, just like she'd done on the street before. She was the ringleader, Immy realized.

Not surprisingly, the girl didn't answer.

"I'm, um, sorry . . . about before. My dad. He says things without thinking. A lot."

"You're really not scared? About the tree?" came a breathy voice. It wasn't the dark-haired girl but one of the others.

The dark-haired girl turned and frowned at her.

Above, one of the boys snorted. "Is that so hard to believe?" He had an American accent. "Why should she be scared?"

Uh-oh. Immy froze. She didn't like how this was going.

The boy swung himself down the two levels of the wooden fort and landed, with a thump, in front of the dark-haired girl. "News flash: not everyone's scared about living with your big old tree."

"I'm not *scared*," the girl snapped back.

"You moved out, didn't you?"

"We needed a bigger house, *Riley*." She practically spat out his name.

"Interesting timing on the move, *Caitlyn*."

If it was even possible, the girl's expression was now even more thunderous-looking than before— her cheeks red and her jaw hard. She took a step toward Immy, her eyes filled with fury. "So you're saying my family's stupid? We're mad. Crazy?"

"No!" Immy held her hands up. "It's just . . . my dad says things like that all the time. He didn't mean it. Honestly. He just has this thing about superstitions and . . ." She trailed off, realizing Caitlyn wasn't listening.

"What would you know?" Caitlyn said. "What would you know about anything? You've been here for five minutes. You think it's just an ordinary tree? You wait. You'll see."

Immy's mouth hung open. She didn't know what to say.

"Let's go." Caitlyn turned and flounced off, the other girls following her.

The boy Riley turned to Immy. He had a smirk

on his face that looked like he thought all of this was funny. "This is what happens when you never leave this place." He raised his voice so the departing girls could still hear him. "You spend your whole life crossing the road to avoid a tree."

Caitlyn ignored him.

Meanwhile, Immy wanted to dig a hole and bury herself in it.

"She really couldn't be more annoying if she tried. She's always going on about that tree. Everyone is. This whole village is insane. So, did your parents come here for work?" Riley asked.

Still in shock, it took Immy a second or two to register his question. "Um, yes. My mum. At the hospital."

"Yeah, mine, too." He clambered back up the wooden fort to his friends and their stash of berries.

Immy's eyes tracked his journey upward. "Well, see you . . ." she said. He honestly didn't seem to realize he'd just wrecked her whole life. He *and* her dad.

Busy with his friends again, Riley didn't answer, and after a moment or two, Immy dragged her heels back across the green to her dad, who was sitting on a bench.

"How did it go?" he asked her.

"Oh, great, thanks," she replied. "We're all the best of friends. We even made plans to meet up at the witch burning tonight."

9
Jean Drops By

The delivery truck with all of the linen and dishes came, and the family spent the rest of the afternoon attempting to find places to fit everything, which wasn't easy in the tiny cottage. All evening, Immy found herself humming the tune of that strange song in her head over and over again. She worried she'd have horrible dreams about the tree, and she shut the curtains as tightly as she could. However, she was so tired that she fell into a deep sleep in no time. When she woke, she couldn't remember having any dreams at all and the song was gone.

After a late breakfast, Immy and her parents sat

around the kitchen table, planning a massive grocery list. It was around ten when Immy caught sight of something moving in the garden out of the corner of her eye. She craned her neck to take another look. It was an old lady with silvery-white hair and a peach-colored cardigan. She closed the little wooden gate behind her that Immy and her dad had gone through yesterday—the one that led into the adjoining garden with the beautiful roses. Immy could see she was holding something in her hands.

"There's someone . . ." Immy began to say, but she stopped, her mouth remaining open, as she saw the woman approach the tree. She watched as the woman reached out, touched the lower knot on the tree, and then took a moment to tuck a white rose in it. Another white rose. Just like the one that had been stuck in the knot yesterday. ". . . in our garden," Immy finally finished her sentence.

Her parents stood, and Immy's dad went over to open the French doors.

"Hello?" Immy's dad called out.

"Oh, hello there!" The woman continued toward them. Immy could see now that she carried a plate and a little porcelain jug. "I'm Jean, from the house behind yours. I'm sorry for barging in, but I wanted to bring you a cake as a housewarming gift."

"Oh, how kind of you!" Immy's mum beamed. "I'm Katie, and this is Andrew and our daughter, Imogen."

"Immy," said Immy.

"Do come in," Immy's mum said. "We were just going to make another cup of tea. Would you like one? A slice of cake would be perfect."

"Tea would be lovely, thank you," Jean said, stepping in through the French doors.

"We were just admiring your garden yesterday," Immy's dad said. "Stunning roses you have there."

Jean nodded. "Thank you. They do come up well this time of the year if you look after them properly. Now, Immy. Let me show you how this cake works. It's a bit of a special one. I'll get you to do it. I'm a bit shaky at eighty-two, I'm afraid, and it's best done with a steady hand!"

Jean placed the cake on the table and handed the little blue-and-white jug to Immy, who wondered if she should pass it to her mother. As a surgeon, she surely had the steadiest hand of anyone in the room. But Jean seemed to trust her with the jug.

"You simply need to pour the syrup on very slowly," Jean told her, watching her closely.

Carefully, Immy leaned over and began to pour the syrup from the jug onto the top of the cake. She thought it would simply pool around the bottom. It didn't. Instead, the cake began to drink up the clear liquid thirstily.

"It's warm, you see," Jean explained. "It sucks all the elderflower syrup into itself."

"Oh, how special!" Immy's mum said, and as Immy finished pouring the syrup, she glanced up and could see how happy her mother was. She was getting everything she wanted. The warm, cozy cottage in the picturesque village, the elderly neighbor who grew gorgeous roses and made fancy cakes. Pity about the horrible tree and the fact that half the village probably hated them already. "I'll just put the kettle on and grab a knife and some plates." Her mother moved off, smile still wide on her face. Immy watched her go. *Things could be worse*, she thought. *Jean could have brought banana bread.* She couldn't stand banana bread.

The elderflower cake was duly devoured and washed down with tea.

"This is simply divine," Immy's mum said, staring at her fork as if she couldn't believe her luck.

It really was. The cake was sticky and crumbly and delicious.

"The elderflowers are from my own garden," Jean said. "I can give you some if you like, along with the recipe."

Immy's dad laughed. "I don't think there'd be any point in that!"

Jean looked a bit shocked, but Immy's mum only chuckled. "It's true. I don't bake."

"And Dad sometimes bakes but shouldn't," Immy added.

Her father made a face at her before turning back to Jean. "However, if you need some excellent heart surgery, pop over anytime and Katie will surely oblige."

"Oh! You're a heart surgeon? I find surgery fascinating! I used to assist in surgery myself sometimes for my husband, though his specialty was animals. He was a vet, you see."

After all this talk of jobs and cooking, Immy couldn't wait any longer. "You're the person who puts the flowers in the tree. The roses. You stick them in there. Why?"

Everyone turned to look at Immy.

"Sorry," she continued. "I just ... had to know." She could barely believe anyone was brave enough to touch that tree.

Immy's parents went to protest, but Jean only waved a hand. "I hope it's all right. I do it every day. I have for ... oh ... seventy-one years now, it would be. I've hardly ever missed a day. When there are no roses to be had, I use holly."

Immy's mum looked confused.

"They have told you? About the two girls?" Jean said.

"Not much." Immy spoke for the three of them. "Not enough."

Jean nodded. "It's why I put a flower in the tree every day. To remember both those girls, but particularly the one that was taken last. Elizabeth her name was. My friend Elizabeth."

"You knew her?" Immy's mum asked.

"Oh, yes. She was a lovely girl. My dearest friend. She had the greenest eyes. Quite mesmerizing, they were. She came when the bombing started in London — to live with her aunt and uncle in Lavender Cottage. The cottage has been in the family for generations, you know. Ever since it was first built. Anyway, they couldn't have children of their own, but they loved having Elizabeth with them. They doted on her, and Elizabeth took to the village like a duck to water—she adored not being cooped up like she had been in London. She and I were as thick as thieves almost instantly. I should think the gate nearly came off its hinges, we were in each other's garden so often! But then she was taken. On VE Day." Seeing Immy's blank expression, she explained. "Victory in Europe Day, Immy. The day the Nazis surrendered. May 8, 1945, it was. I'll never forget it. For so many reasons." She looked wistful.

"It must have been awful. Having a child in the village disappear," Immy's dad said. "I can't imagine."

Jean nodded. "It makes my heart clench just to think about it. As a child, to lose my friend was bad enough, but now that I'm a mother . . . oh, it doesn't bear thinking about."

Immy's parents both nodded.

Jean took a deep breath. "Still, it's why I've come. To warn you about the tree."

10

Jean's Warning

"Now, I'm not here to fill your head with nonsense. I just want you to know the facts. Elizabeth was here. So here. Young and very alive. I can vouch for it. And then, the evening before her eleventh birthday, she simply . . . disappeared. In exactly the same way as we'd always been told the other girl had. Bridget her name was. She was taken on the evening before her eleventh birthday as well."

"So the two girls who were taken were related?" Immy's mother said.

"Yes, they were."

Immy's mum pushed her plate away from her a little. "I'm sorry, but surely you don't think the tree really took your friend? It must have been someone who lived here. Statistically, I would say that it was someone known to her."

"I know it's not possible, and yet"—Jean glanced outside—"I believe it's true."

"The knot," Immy spoke up. "Did it really appear just like that? Overnight?"

Jean nodded. "It most certainly did."

A shadow passed over the room, which darkened considerably. Immy gulped.

"News gets around here, so when I heard you'd moved in and had a daughter with a significant birthday coming up . . . I was worried. But then I told myself things are different. The house, well, it's nothing to do with your family, is it? And you'll have been here such a short amount of time when . . ." Her eyes moved to Immy. It was obvious everyone was thinking about her upcoming birthday. "Oh, I've said too much. It's not my place, is it? I had to tell you, though. I had to make absolutely sure you knew." Jean's hands, with their large knuckles, twisted worriedly.

Immy had expected her parents to be angry, but they weren't. Instead, her mother nodded as if she were taking Jean's advice to heart. She glanced at Immy's dad. "To tell you the truth, we've been thinking about a weekend trip to Paris. Maybe we'll go for Immy's birthday. So Immy doesn't worry. And to keep everyone in the village happy."

Jean brightened with this, sitting up straighter, her face lightening. "What an excellent idea. You'll love Paris, Immy! The museums, the street cafés, just wandering around. Not to mention it would be a nice break after the first weeks of school. You've got one more week off, don't you?"

Immy nodded.

"Back to school next Monday. I know that because my daughter Claire works at the village school. But I've kept you all too long." Jean stood. "You've just moved in, and you're a busy family with things to do."

"Only groceries," Immy said, thinking she'd much rather hear anything else Jean had to say about the tree. She wanted to know more. So much more. Like what had happened when everyone realized Elizabeth had gone missing. What the police had said. Who the police thought had taken her. Who the village thought had taken her.

"Ah, but you'll be wanting your dinner tonight, Immy, which is why you need to help your parents with the groceries now," Jean told her. "It was lovely meeting you all. Thank you for the tea."

Immy's parents stood as well.

"No, thank *you* for the cake, Jean," Immy's dad said. "It really was delicious."

Jean was already at the French doors. She didn't stop but simply waved a hand over her shoulder and was gone.

The threesome watched her go. As she passed by the tree, she reached out and touched the knot again — the one with the rose in it.

Immy's mum waited until Jean had finished crossing the garden and the little gate had closed behind her. Then she shook her head. "It's not some silly story to her, is it? She really believes it's true. She really believes the tree took those two girls."

The next morning, Immy woke to the sound of the shower and creaking on the stairs. She tried to go back to sleep, but now that she'd been wrenched from her dreams, she couldn't. All she could think about was the curtains covering the window and, behind the curtains . . . the tree.

Without warning, the song entered her head again, and she realized she'd heard it in her dreams, too. She tried to push it away, but it remained there, going around and around in circles. What was it? Where had it come from? She must have heard it somewhere for it to have stuck like this.

After a few more minutes, Immy got up and made her way downstairs. She found her father sitting at the kitchen table and her mother whirling around like a tornado, getting ready for work. She'd almost forgotten it was Monday morning.

"Ah, there she is," her mother said, a triangle of toast in her hand. "An email came in last night. You can get your uniforms this morning. They've sent a list." She pointed the toast at Immy's dad. "What did we decide?"

He fished around on the table for a piece of paper and read from it. "Three skirts, three shirts, one sweater, and as many socks as the washing machine can possibly eat. They'll be in the school hall starting at nine this morning."

Immy groaned, thinking about all the trying on of clothes she was going to have to do.

"You'll get to meet some of the other kids, I expect," her mum said.

Immy looked at her dad. Thanks to him, she already had. Obviously he hadn't said anything to her mother.

"Well, I have to run," Immy's mum said, pausing to down the last of her coffee. "Sure you don't need the car?"

"No, we'll putter around here today. Get uniforms and so on. Search the internet for ways to poison trees without being detected . . ."

"Dad!" Immy said.

Her parents both laughed.

"I'll see you tonight." Her mother picked up the car keys off the table, blew them both a kiss, and was out the door in a flash.

Her dad stood. "You get yourself some cereal. I'll have a shower and we'll be first in line at the school, okay?"

"Okay," Immy said, heading for the kitchen.

She waited until she heard her dad's footsteps on the stairs. And then she went back over to the table and grabbed his phone.

His comment about the internet had given her an idea.

11

At School

Keeping one ear out for the sound of her father's footsteps, Immy began to tap out letters on his phone. Her fingers felt slow and awkward as she tried to type quickly. It wasn't that her father would mind her using his phone; it was more what she was using it for. She knew her parents wouldn't like it if they thought she was too worried about the tree. Every so often, she glanced out the French doors. It felt like the tree was watching her.

The first search term she entered was "evil trees." It wasn't very helpful. All that came up was information about some sort of online role-playing game and silly pictures of trees with red eyes and flailing branches for arms. After a few minutes she gave up and tried something else. This time she typed the name of the village and the names Bridget and Elizabeth. She expected pages and pages of information to come up, but there wasn't much at all. A few newspaper articles popped up on historical blogs to do with the area. There was some basic information about Elizabeth and how she had gone missing on VE Day, in 1945, and not much else. There was only the vaguest mention of Bridget, one article saying that the village locals recalled the story of a girl who went missing at the same age in 1795.

With her next search, Immy tried to be more specific. She typed "ancient tree England." Something came up about sacred Celtic trees, and she skimmed the information as fast as she could. The site spoke about ash, oak, apple, elder, hazel, yew, and alder trees at length, but it didn't mention mulberry trees at all.

Frowning, Immy put her dad's phone back down on the table. She looked outside at the tree, which didn't need evil red eyes to glare back at her. As she stared at it, her heart thumping away in her chest, she heard the shower turn off upstairs. She jumped up and ran to the kitchen to get her cereal.

At just after nine, Immy and her dad walked the short distance to the village school and went through the large green metal gates, which had been unlocked and pushed back. They passed by a bike rack and saw a couple of other parents and kids rounding the corner of a brick building beyond.

"That way." Immy pointed, and they followed the other people. Both she and her father dragged their heels a little. Surely what her dad had said would have been gossiped about in the village by now.

When they rounded the corner of the building, Immy could see a bunch of kids playing in a playground, which had some wooden climbing equipment and some monkey bars and swings and so on. The kids weren't the ones from the village green, she was pleased to see.

Immy and her dad kept following the group from before, who had just entered a door that seemed to lead into a long building that looked like a hall.

It *was* a hall. Inside it, voices reverberated around the room, with its high ceiling and wooden floor. A long table had been set up with lots of gray-and-blue uniforms on it—gray skirts and trousers and shorts and blue shirts and polos.

Immy and her dad approached two women who were standing behind the table sorting out pieces of paper.

"Hello," he said. "I'm Andrew, and this is Imogen. Immy's starting at the school next week, and we've come to buy her uniforms."

"Oh, how lovely!" one of the women gushed. "A new girl! We don't have many girls at the school. Certainly not in the upper years. There aren't many in the village of course, and . . ."

The other woman turned and gave her a knowing look. "This is the family from Lavender Cottage."

"Oh!" The first woman started, her eyes wide. There was a long pause. "Oh, I see."

The two women stared at Immy's dad.

"I, ah . . ." he started. "I'm afraid I put my foot in my mouth the other day and—"

The first woman cut him off. "We find that three of everything works well." Her voice was curt. "Size twelve should be right. Take this skirt and blouse and try them on in the first office down the corridor, just beyond the doors there. Then you can be on your way."

* * *

Immy tried on the clothes in silence. Neither she nor her dad said a word before opening the office door.

"Right. So all of this, plus two more blouses and two more skirts," her dad said.

"And socks." Immy's voice was expressionless.

"Yes, socks, of course. Why don't you go outside to the playground while I finish this up? There were some kids out there before."

Immy didn't want to go out to the playground, but she also didn't want to stay with her dad.

"You really should try to meet a few of them before next week. Invite some of them over for a playdate."

"I don't think anyone's going to be lining up to come over. Not when they won't even walk on our side of the street." *And when you've made them all hate us,* she added in her head.

"Oh, dear. Maybe we should have taken that apartment after all . . ."

Immy shrugged and followed her dad as they made their way back into the hall. Maybe they should have, but it was too late now.

As they entered the hall, Immy noticed that a

woman with dark hair had joined the two women from before. The three of them stood, their heads bent in toward one another, their hands moving as fast as their mouths. It was obvious what they were talking about. As Immy and her dad approached, one of the group noticed them and alerted the others. When the woman with the dark hair lifted her head, Immy took in her deep brown eyes and realized she looked a lot like Caitlyn from the village green.

Oh, great.

Her dad was so on his own for this one.

Immy turned on her heel. "I'm going outside."

12

Next in Line

Immy sat on a log that she guessed was supposed to be a balance beam and chatted with a girl named Ava, who was in the year below her. Kids were running all around them, and Immy noticed that most of them were boys. The woman at the table in the hall had been right. There really *weren't* many girls in this village.

After a few minutes, Ava's mother called her into the hall, and Immy was left sitting by herself. It wasn't long before she heard it—the song. Her back stiffened. But wait. This time . . . this time it wasn't in her head. Someone was singing it out aloud. It was more than one person, she realized—there were two or three. Just as she swiveled on the log, a woman's voice called out.

"Girls! Come here. Right now, please."

It was Caitlyn the woman was talking to. Caitlyn and the two other girls. As she watched, they shuffled across the playground to the woman, who was standing near what Immy guessed were the classrooms. She carried a pile of books under one arm and was obviously a teacher.

"I do *not* want to hear that rhyme at this school. That tree is hundreds of years old and of great historical significance. Fear, ignorance, and hate can lead to terrible things, and it's silly talk like yours that makes people destroy things. I sincerely hope you're not going to start the year off on the wrong foot."

There was silence.

"Are you, Caitlyn? Zara? Erin?"

"No, miss," all three girls said at the same time. Caitlyn's gaze slid to meet Immy's, and the look she gave her! If she'd hated Immy before, she was out to get her now.

"Good. Well, off you go, then. Into the hall. I'm sure your parents are looking for you."

All three girls trudged off toward the hall in

silence. The woman waited until they'd entered. Then she turned, and her gaze met Immy's for a moment. She smiled a small smile, and it was then that Immy realized the woman knew who she was. She knew she was living in Lavender Cottage.

Was there anyone in this village who *didn't* know they'd moved in? Immy doubted it.

Immy stood and lifted a hand in an awkward wave, but the woman with the books had already turned and was making her way back inside.

Immy was still standing there, in exactly the same position, when one of the girls reappeared from the hall. Not Caitlyn, but one of the other two — either Zara or Erin according to the woman who'd told them off. The first thing the girl did was check for the teacher. Seeing she wasn't there, she shifted her gaze to where Immy had been sitting. She looked a bit taken aback when she realized Immy hadn't left.

The girl hesitated and glanced back toward the hall. Immy guessed that her mother had sent her outside. Now she was trapped.

Before the girl could disappear somewhere else, Immy started across the playground toward her. She had to find out what that rhyme was. And why the teacher had been angry with them for singing it.

The girl's eyes widened when she realized Immy was coming straight toward her. She checked behind herself quickly, as if to see if help was coming. Immy guessed she didn't know what to do without Caitlyn leading the way.

Immy stopped right in front of her. "What's that song you keep singing?"

"I . . ." The girl took a step backward.

"I want to know," Immy insisted. Her stomach was churning. She didn't like arguments or fighting with people. She could feel unexpected tears welling up behind her eyes, and she gulped, trying to push them away. "Tell me!"

"You really want to know?"

"Yes! Now!"

"But the teacher said . . ."

"You didn't seem so worried about teachers when you had your friends with you. Now hurry up and tell me."

A final backward glance told the girl that no one was coming to save her.

"Well?"

"Okay! Okay, already! It's . . . it's about the tree. People have sung it here for . . . I don't know . . . forever, I suppose. It goes like this: 'Do naught wrong by the mulberry tree, or she'll take your daughters . . . one, two, three. In the dead of night, spirited away, never to see an eleventh birthday.'" Her cheeks red, she rushed through the words, then waited for Immy's reaction.

Immy stood frozen, her mind working backward. "It can't be," she said. The rhyme. She'd heard it in her head even before they'd decided to rent Lavender Cottage. No one from the village had told it to her. It had just appeared.

In her dream.

Girls had been singing it in her dream.

The girl looked at her like she was crazy. "What do you mean it can't be?"

"I . . ."

"Don't you get it?" The girl took a step forward. "'She'll take your daughters . . . one, two, three.' Two have already been taken. *You're the third girl.*"

* * *

Immy and her dad started the walk home with their big bag of uniforms, neither of them saying very much.

"Speak to any of the kids?" her dad eventually asked her.

Immy wasn't sure what to say. Should she tell him about the rhyme? She decided not to, because she wasn't sure what to think about it herself yet. "I met a nice girl named Ava. She's in the year below me."

"Good."

They walked the rest of the short way in silence as Immy thought about the teacher who'd told the girls off. The woman's words kept playing over and over again in Immy's mind. *Fear, ignorance, and hate can lead to terrible things,* she'd said. Immy's brow creased as she struggled to make sense of this. And, on top of that, the rhyme, which had started to repeat itself in her head again now that she knew the words, distracting her and muddling her train of thought: *Do naught wrong by the mulberry tree, or she'll take your daughters . . . one, two, three. In the dead of night, spirited away, never to see an eleventh birthday.*

"What did you say?" Her dad glanced down at her as he held open Lavender Cottage's gate.

"Nothing," Immy said quickly, her breath

catching as she felt the shadow of the tree looming over the back of the house. "I was just . . . singing to myself." She slowed as they walked up the side of the house around to the French doors, where they'd taken to entering and exiting the house.

Her dad let himself in, but Immy remained outside, pretending to tidy up her shoes on the rack. It wasn't until he was out of sight that she dared to look up. The tree was waiting for her, brooding in the blocked-out sky. It was almost as if it were biding its time, tapping its long roots, counting out the seconds until her birthday. Her stomach flip-flopping, she stared at the two knots in its trunk.

She'll take your daughters . . . one, two, three.

The song in her dream was meant to scare her off. It had been a warning. A warning from the tree. They shouldn't have rented the house.

Immy knew then that she had to find out what had really happened to those two girls.

She had to find out the truth.

Or she'd be next.

13

Waiting

While Immy's mum went to work, Immy and her dad spent the rest of the week doing nothing much at all. Her dad kept saying he "really should see to the garden," then never did. After a few days, Immy's mum started making him lists of things to do, and he'd try to do some of those things (or even one) each day. Whenever he'd done something, Immy would tick it off the list and make sure her mother saw it that evening.

"I really should see to the garden," Immy's dad said over lunch on Friday.

Immy looked up from her sandwich. She thought of the list. On it were only three items. These were:

look into Paris trip, cut up vegetables for dinner, and weed the lawn. Immy had already cut up the vegetables herself and ticked the task off. If her mother thought her father had done it, well, what did that matter?

"Let's weed the lawn after lunch," she said to her dad, even though she (a) didn't want to go into the garden and (b) didn't want to spend time with her dad. "I'll help."

"Good idea." He nodded.

The moment her dad had finished his sandwich, Immy slid his plate out from under him. "I'll do the dishes," she said. "You go outside and start the weeding."

She rinsed their plates and stacked the dishwasher as fast as she could, hoping her dad had started the small job that should take only twenty minutes or so.

She'd almost finished when she glanced out the kitchen window to see him sitting on the small brick wall next to the shed, staring off into space, one single weed clasped in his hand. She watched him for a full minute. Then a minute more. He didn't move.

Pushing the dishwasher door closed, Immy moved to the kitchen bench and picked up a small rectangular cardboard box. She opened it and pulled out two silver-foil packets. And then she counted her father's pills. There were twelve. There'd been fourteen when he was in the shower this morning, and now there were two fewer. So he was taking his pills. Why weren't they working? He'd been taking them for three weeks now. Pushing the silver packets back inside and closing the box, she pushed it away from her. She grabbed a large garbage bag from under the sink and made her way to the French doors.

"What are you looking at?" she asked her dad from the doorway.

"What? Oh, nothing. Weeds, I suppose."

Immy glanced up at the tree, which menaced the garden, its branches radiating dark thoughts.

Last night she'd started her own list. A secret list. A list of how she might be able to find out more about the tree and stop herself from becoming the third girl who was fated to disappear. She knew she'd have to be careful. If her parents found out she was even thinking about the tree and her birthday, they'd freak out. That's why she'd used her father's phone in secret. But if there wasn't anything much out there on the internet, where else could she get information?

Old newspapers, she supposed. Or maybe people who had lived here when the last girl had gone missing, though they'd be quite old now—like Jean. The school librarian might know something as well.

Her dad nearby, Immy felt brave enough to venture over the threshold and make her way closer to the tree. Two steps, three, four, five . . . if she'd reached out with her hand, she could have touched the trunk. Not that she was going to do *that*. Looking up, her eyes met the tree's branches, jet-black against the sky. As she stared, she could have sworn the branches began to move toward her face. The sensation began to make her feel faint and she shook her head, breaking the spell. It must have been an optical illusion. At least, she hoped it was.

Immy opened the garbage bag in her hand and went over to place it in the middle of the patchy lawn. She then went back to where she'd been before, stooped, and pulled a few random weeds out from the ground beneath the tree. Seeing her efforts, her dad got up and pulled a few more as well, and they began throwing them into a pile on top of the garbage bag.

It didn't take long before they'd developed a kind

of rhythm. Bend down, pluck out the weed, throw the weed . . . bend down, pluck out the weed, throw the weed . . .

Not hearing the rhyme or noticing anything strange, Immy became braver, circling the tree, getting rid of the weeds, short and tall, as she went. She'd gone about halfway around when she noticed some slashes in the tree's thick trunk. She paused for a moment, a weed in her hand, and then took the few steps over that she needed to see them more clearly. She stood on tiptoes and inspected the deep, rough scars. The world seemed to quiet as she concentrated on the marks.

"Dad," she called out, her gaze not moving. "Come and look at this."

"What's that, love?" She could hear him walking over to her and then heard a noise, as if he'd tripped on something. He swore under his breath, but she didn't turn. "Best watch out for that. There's a bit of a dip underneath the grass. There might have been another tree here once," he said when he reached her. He leaned in to see what Immy was looking at. "Hmmm. Looks like someone tried to cut it down at one time or another. Maybe that's why it's so cranky with the world."

The stillness ended with a gust of wind, the tree bristling with the insult.

Immy stepped back, holding her breath.

Her dad went off to pull a few more weeds.

But Immy stayed, staring at the place where, long ago, someone had taken an ax and attempted to slay the tree. *Hack, hack, hack;* she could see exactly where they'd tried to stop it in its tracks. Brutally. Cruelly.

Immy remembered the teacher's words from the playground. *It's silly talk like yours that makes people destroy things,* she had said. Was that what had happened? Believing the tree might take their daughter, too, someone who lived here had tried to chop it down?

The sound of her father throwing weeds into the bag behind her continued as Immy stared upward at the tree's murky branches. She started to feel faint again. Almost like this was a dream. She took a step forward, not because she wanted to but because she felt she had to. She felt like the tree was drawing her closer, just like it had the first time she entered Lavender Cottage. "What happened?" she asked it.

"What happened to you?" Her fingers reached out tentatively to touch the coarse gashes. They hovered above the bark for a moment, uncertain.

Immy was just about to make contact when something like a spark of electricity zapped her, making her pull her hand back sharply. She sucked her breath in, suddenly alert.

It was another clear warning from the tree.

Stay away, girl.

Stay away from me.

14

Lunchtime

The first day of school started off fine. Immy had guessed it would be this way. During lesson times, things would be okay. Yes, there were only four girls in her class (*those* girls — Caitlyn, Zara, Erin — and herself), but during lessons, there was work to do. Everyone was busy. A teacher was present.

It would be lunchtime that would be the hard part.

As the class trekked toward the hall, she tried to fall back and make sure she was as far away from Caitlyn, Zara, and Erin as possible. To make things even worse, she wasn't entirely sure what to do. They had something called school dinners here. Each week the parents paid money, and the school served lunch to the students. That didn't happen back at home.

"Year six!" a voice called out as Immy entered the hall to see chairs and tables had been set out. She groaned a silent groan as she realized there'd been no point in dawdling—she was going to have to line up with the other kids in her year. Reluctantly, she ran over to grab a tray and some cutlery with some of the other kids from her class.

As they approached the servers, Immy copied the boy in front of her and ended up with a tray with macaroni and cheese, a baked potato, some corn, a slice of melon, and a box of apple juice. She followed him over to the tables, where he veered off and took the last seat at a table of twelve. The next-closest table—and the only other one she could see with a 6 on it—already had Caitlyn, Zara, and Erin sitting at it.

Immy's shoulders sagged as she realized what she was going to have to do.

Riley, the boy from the village green, stopped to see what she was looking at. "Lucky for us, lunch is only fifteen minutes," he said.

With a sigh, Immy followed him and sat down, bracing herself for what would probably be the longest fifteen minutes of her life. She put her tray down a bit too hard, and the three girls, who'd been chatting, all looked up at the same time.

Immy ignored them, sat down, and focused on her lunch. She didn't lift her eyes from her tray, not even when she knew they were whispering about her.

It felt like forever before the kids in the hall started to move off to scrape their plates and stack their trays.

Immy followed their lead but then realized there was still another half hour of recess to go before they would head back into the classroom. She went to the bathroom and took a lot of time washing her hands. Hovering around the door to the playground, she could see Caitlyn, Zara, and Erin by the monkey bars. She recognized Ava, the girl she'd spoken to when she'd come to buy her uniforms, but Ava was playing hopscotch with some of the younger girls, and Immy could only imagine what Caitlyn's crew would say if she tried something like that. She also saw Riley, who she thought seemed nice, but he was heading off with a group of boys to play soccer.

She thought back to her old school in Sydney, where she had friends — friends she hoped to return to before too long. What would she have done if she hadn't been able to sit with them? There'd been a lot of lunchtime activities at her old school — coding club, chess club, Amnesty International. But this school was tiny. They probably wouldn't have things like that here. It didn't take her long to remember another place of refuge, however. And she knew this school had one, because her teacher had pointed it out to her this morning.

Immy turned and made her way toward the library.

When she pushed open the doors to the small library, Immy was pleased to see that there were several other kids in there. Two were lounging around on beanbags, reading. A few others were sitting at a table, playing a board game.

She breathed a sigh of relief. She could handle

fifteen minutes of lunch and half an hour of recess in here. Things would be all right.

"Hello," someone said, approaching her. "It's Imogen, isn't it?"

"Immy." Immy nodded. It was the woman from the playground. The one who'd told Caitlyn, Zara, and Erin off.

"I'm Mrs. Garland, the school librarian. I'm Jean Merritt's daughter. Jean who lives behind you."

"Oh!" Immy remembered Jean telling her that her daughter worked at the village school. "Hello."

"I was wondering when you'd come in. Why don't you have a look around? If you have any questions, just let me know."

"All right," Immy said. "Thanks."

Mrs. Garland bustled off back to her desk and sat down at her computer.

After a moment or two, Immy moved off, taking herself through the shelves, picking out books here and there and flipping through the pages. She did this for the next twenty minutes or so, watching Mrs. Garland out of the corner of her eye as she went. She couldn't stop thinking about what she'd said to the girls, and she wondered how much she knew about the tree—probably as much as Jean did, which was a lot.

It was strange, but the tree had seemed a bit quieter since the strange jolt it had given her. And since she'd found out about the rhyme. Maybe that's all it wanted? To be left alone? For a moment, she considered letting things be, but then she thought of the tree outside her bedroom window and shuddered. There were only five more minutes of lunchtime left. She had to be brave and ask what she wanted to ask. On Immy's list of how to find out more about the tree, one of the possible information sources she'd written down was the school librarian. The school librarian's mother living right behind the mulberry tree was sheer luck. This was too good a chance to pass up.

Mrs. Garland was sitting at her desk. Immy sidled on over, trying to look casual.

"Oh, hello again, Immy." Mrs. Garland looked up as she approached. "How can I help you?"

"Well," Immy said. "I was wondering if you have any books about mulberries."

Mrs. Garland's eyebrows shot up. "Hmmm . . . that's very specific. No, I don't think we do."

"I was wondering . . . did you grow up in the house behind ours?"

"Oh, no." Mrs. Garland shook her head. "It was my grandparents' house. My mother only moved back there when she sold our family home and needed something smaller. But she grew up there."

Immy wasn't sure how much she could ask. "When she knew her friend Elizabeth?" She lowered her voice.

Mrs. Garland shifted in her seat. "Well, yes . . ."

"And the people Elizabeth lived with, where are they now?"

"They were older, so they died some time ago." She hesitated. "The house was kept in the family, though. It went to their nephew—Caitlyn's father."

Immy glanced out toward the playground. She paused to think for a moment before continuing. "What you said the other day to the girls in the playground. I've been thinking about that. What did you mean?"

"You heard me?"

Immy nodded.

"Well, let's see. I suppose I was trying to explain

to the girls that people are often afraid of what they don't truly understand. You can see it throughout history. The banning or burning of books, the persecution of certain religions, of races . . ."

Immy thought about the marks on the tree. "Do *you* think the tree is evil?" Her eyes were glued to Mrs. Garland.

"I . . . I suppose I think nothing's ever truly evil—all good or all bad, all black or all white. Life isn't like that, is it?"

For some reason, Immy's thoughts turned to Bob. She saw him as something blacker than black. He'd been wrong—wrong to drive that car. That's all there was to it. Immy shrugged, not wanting to think about this.

"You know, if you're interested in gardening, you should join our allotment club," Mrs. Garland said, quickly changing the subject.

"What's an allotment?"

"Of course, I completely forgot. It's quite an English thing. Maybe you'd call it a community garden? Do you have those in Australia?"

Immy nodded. She knew what a community garden was.

"Well, the school has an allotment, and I run the club. We meet there on Wednesday and Friday afternoons, after school. We grow all sorts of things. Carrots, potatoes, herbs, rhubarb. The first meeting will be this Friday. Do you think you'd like to join?"

"I'm not sure," Immy said as the bell rang.

Mrs. Garland stood. "Well, you think about it, and I'll remind you later in the week if I see you."

"All right." Immy started toward the door. "I'll be here in the library, that's for sure."

15
At the Pool

The week continued in pretty much the same way. The tree remained silent, but Immy knew it was watching her. She could feel it. At school, there were lessons, first break, lessons, lunch/hide in the library time, lessons, and then home. First break wasn't too bad, because you were allowed to stay in the classroom and read a book or draw if you wanted to. When it came to lunch, Immy simply scarfed down her meal as fast as she could and ran for the library. After three days of it, she figured she could stand doing this for a year. Hopefully her family would return to Australia after that. She guessed whether they stayed here depended entirely on her mum's work.

And whether her dad would ever work again.

After quizzing Mrs. Garland, she'd tried to find out even more information about the tree. She'd asked her dad if they could go to the big library, in Cambridge itself, but he said it was a half-hour drive and that you then had to park in some sort of lot and take a special bus in. They'd have to wait until they had some free time on a weekend. Immy knew what that meant. It was all going to be too hard, as most things were for her father these days.

On Friday, things were a bit different because Immy's class was going to start swimming lessons for the year. Immy quite liked swimming. In Sydney, she'd been taking lessons at a university pool since she was six months old, and, slowly, she had worked her way up to two squad sessions per week during the summer. Her dad used to swim at the same time, but he hadn't done that in a while.

Immy wasn't a great swimmer, but she enjoyed it. Even though there were plenty of kids who could swim way faster than she could, she didn't care. She still liked to do all the laps written up on the squad whiteboard. She liked the fact that, in the pool, she could just concentrate on putting one arm over the other and practice breathing at the right time. She didn't have to think about anything else. Afterward, her dad would get a coffee, and Immy would get an ice pop, and they'd sit on the café's sun-soaked, wide wooden deck. Here they'd watch the swimmers go up and down, up and down, the tall palm trees swaying in the background.

It was raining when Immy's class got off the minibus at the small sports complex that housed the pool. Immy followed the other kids inside and then halted when she caught her first glimpse of where they'd be swimming.

"Oh" was all she could say.

This wasn't the university pool.

This pool was indoors. It was only twenty-five meters long, and it *stank* of chlorine. The air was thick and heavy, and it was hard to breathe.

They continued on to the changing rooms. As Immy entered, she tensed, realizing it was going to be difficult to avoid Caitlyn and her friends in the small space. Immy swung her swimming bag onto a bench on the opposite side of the changing room from them and proceeded to get changed as fast as she could.

She was about halfway through pulling her

swimsuit on when Caitlyn began humming the rhyme about the mulberry tree under her breath.

Immy's worry turned into a sudden flare of anger. She was sick of Caitlyn. Yes, her dad had said something dumb, but when was she going to let it go? She was so mean. It was as if living in the shadow of the tree had made her a sour, bitter person.

Maybe that was it. Maybe it had.

There was more than one voice humming along by the time Immy grabbed her goggles and made her way out to the pool. Immy didn't stop to check who it was. Probably Zara or Erin, she guessed.

The instructor waited until their teacher had counted heads and made sure everyone was present. She then lined them up in four groups behind the four lanes, according to a sheet on her clipboard. Immy guessed the groups were sorted according to their swimming ability. Her dad had had to fill out a form, saying how good a swimmer she was and what she could and couldn't do.

Unfortunately, she was grouped with not only Caitlyn but Erin, too—the girl who'd told her the words of the rhyme. As they joined her, Riley's name was also called out, as well as another boy,

Will, who she hadn't really spoken to yet.

The humming started again.

It continued as the instructor told them their group was going to begin by swimming a relay. Any stroke they liked—up and back, fifty meters each.

"Who wants to go first?" the instructor asked.

"I will," Immy volunteered. Anything to get away from that humming.

"Great," the instructor said. "Up you get."

Immy climbed up on the block and pulled her goggles down.

"Ready . . . set . . . go."

Immy dived in and swam. The water was too warm and felt soupy, but she didn't care. She just swam, concentrating on one arm following the other and on taking deep breaths.

She did a tumble turn, swam back again, and then slammed her hand against the tiles when she reached the wall once more. Immy looked up through foggy goggles to see a pair of feet narrowly miss her head as someone dived in.

Caitlyn.

Puffing, she pulled herself out the water and rejoined the others in her group.

Who were all staring at her.

"What?" she finally said.

"That was . . . amazing," Will told her.

Beside him, Erin's eyes were wide. "You're really good." Her gaze flicked nervously to Caitlyn, halfway up the pool, as if she might be able to hear.

"Yeah, you're pretty fast." Riley nodded. "Faster than me, that's for sure."

"And he's the fastest in the whole school," Will said.

Immy frowned. "But I'm not some amazing swimmer. Back at home, I'm just . . . well, average, really."

"Maybe it's all the swimming away from sharks you have to do in Australia." Riley grinned. "Makes you quicker."

When the lesson was over, Immy raced to throw her clothes on so she could get back on the bus. She slumped down into a seat near the front, but there was no avoiding Caitlyn, who bent down and hissed at her as she walked past.

"You really think you're better than everyone in the whole village, don't you?" she said.

As Immy looked up at her, she caught something

in Caitlyn's expression. Something gnarled and dark and resentful that reminded her of the tree again. Saying nothing, Immy rolled her eyes, turned, and stared out the window. If she lived in Caitlyn's house for too long, would she end up like that, too? She was beginning to regret talking her parents into renting Lavender Cottage. Maybe they *should* have waited and looked at places in town, where she could have gone to a bigger school. Found somewhere with a tree that wouldn't eat her on her birthday.

She paused. Did she really regret her decision? The thing was, there was something about that tree. She wanted to know more. Had to. Not just because she was still a bit worried it might steal her away, too, but because she wanted to know what had happened to those two girls. So, no, she wasn't sorry they were living there. Not really. Finding out more about the tree was worth it, even if it meant putting up with horrible Caitlyn.

Slowly, everyone else filed onto the bus. And of course no one would sit next to her. As more and more kids got on, the seat beside Immy began to look glaringly vacant. That is, until someone dropped into it with a *whump*.

"So," Riley said. "School, huh? Having fun yet?"

"Oh, yeah. I'm loving it," Immy answered with a snort.

"Look on the bright side," Riley said. "At least you're still here. At least the tree hasn't *taken you in the night* yet." He waggled his fingers in her face and made some spooky noises.

Riley had to be the only person in the whole village who wasn't scared of talking about the tree. Unfortunately for her, this was because he was new to the village as well. This meant he wouldn't know as much about the tree as the kids whose families had lived here for generations did. Immy thought of something. "Do you ever go to the library in town?"

"You mean into the city? Into Cambridge?"

"No." Immy shook her head. "Into . . ." She frowned, trying to remember the name of the nearest town.

"St. Isles?" Riley guessed as the bus took off with a jerk.

"Yep, that one."

"Sure. I catch the bus to the library all the time with my mom. We go most Saturdays."

"The bus?"

"It goes from just up the road from your house. It takes about fifteen minutes."

"And it stops near the library?"

"Right outside it. Why?"

Immy considered Riley for a moment. He could be trusted, she thought. "I want to find out more." She lowered her voice. "About the tree. Its history."

"Hey, you know what they have there? This whole big wall of framed photographs. Old ones. The black-and-white kind. They've got some sort of historical society that the librarian is always trying to get my mom to join. She's sort of interested because our house is so old and everything. You should go. To the library, I mean."

Immy sighed. "I can't. I can't tell my parents I want to go. They'd freak out if they thought I was thinking about the tree too much. I know they would."

"Well, *we* could go."

"What? On our own?"

"Why not? It wouldn't take too much time. What could go wrong?"

Immy laughed. "My dad could kill me. That's what."

"He wouldn't even know. The librarian's name is Mrs. Marsh. She'd definitely help you. She loves it when we ask her about any history stuff. She can go on all day! Look, when we get back to school, I'll write down my number and give it to you. If you want to go on Saturday afternoon, just call me. Mom's going to London for the weekend, and my dad wouldn't notice if I said I was going over to someone's house for a couple hours."

Immy just stared at him as the bus pulled inside the school gates and parked in the small lot. He was living in a dreamland. There was no way this was going to happen. Ever.

As they filed out of the bus and walked back into the school, they passed by the library, and Immy saw Mrs. Garland talking to a student through the library windows. The library in Cambridge, or even in St. Isles, might not happen, but maybe she could try to get some more information from Mrs. Garland?

After lunch, she made her way to the library.

"Mrs. Garland," Immy said as soon as she got there. "Is the allotment club still on this afternoon? I might give it a go after all."

16

The Allotment Club

"So I'm going to this thing at four o'clock," Immy told her dad as they walked home from school that afternoon.

"Cocktail party?"

"Very funny. The school's allotment club. It's like a community garden."

"Oh! You mean the allotments next to the village green?"

"I guess so." That's where Mrs. Garland had told her they were.

"Well, that's a good idea." He looked up at the sky, which was blue and streaked with feathery white clouds. "Nice afternoon for it. You know what? I might even do a bit of gardening myself. Finally get out that hedge trimmer."

"Sure," Immy said, doubting that would actually happen.

"No, I mean it."

"Okay."

Immy dumped her schoolbag at home and grabbed a snack. Amazingly, her dad went out to the shed and fished out the hedge trimmer and some other gardening tools.

He popped his head inside the French doors. "I'll walk you down to the allotment, and then I'll get started."

"Mmm," Immy said, her mouth full of apple. The tools might have left the shed, but she still didn't believe the gardening thing would actually happen.

The pair set out for the allotment with time to spare.

"Let's go the long way," Immy's dad suggested as they started along the footpath. "There's a side gate that leads onto the village green."

"Okay." Immy shrugged, following her dad.

It was only a short distance inside the gate that they stumbled across the tree.

"Whoa." Immy's dad stopped to stare up at it. "It might be smaller than ours, but that's the kind of mulberry tree you *want* in your garden."

Immy gulped as she stared up at the tree. Not out of fear this time, like the tree made her do in her own back garden, but because the mulberry tree's clusters of blue-red berries looked so plump and delicious that she could already taste them. Her dad was right. This was a completely different sort of mulberry. Instead of being ancient and wizened and cranky, it stood peacefully in its place, leaves fluttering gently in the breeze—tall and green and serene. As she inspected it, she remembered something—the very first time she'd been on the village green, Riley and his friends had been eating berries out of an upturned cap. It must have been mulberries they'd been eating. These mulberries.

Her eyes still glued to the tree's fruit-laden branches, Immy took her hat off and handed it to her father. "Let's load up and we'll eat them as we go."

* * *

They were still munching berries when they got to the allotment.

"Isn't it lovely?" her dad said as they let themselves inside the little blue wooden gate that fitted snugly into the wire fence.

It *was* pretty. There were several raised rectangular garden beds with rows of herbs and lettuces, and the borders consisted of all sorts of blooming flowers—reds and purples and pinks and yellows. At the end was a blue wooden shed, painted the same color as the gate.

Mrs. Garland waved and started over to greet them.

"Quick; have I got mulberries all over my face?" Immy asked her dad.

"Looking good." He brushed out her hat and popped it back on her head.

While Immy's dad and Mrs. Garland were chatting, some of the other kids from school came inside the gate.

Immy knew only two of them—Riley and, she was surprised to see, Erin.

Amazingly, without Zara or Caitlyn by her side.

The moment she saw Immy, Erin looked nervous. It didn't take long before she sidled up to Immy.

"Don't tell Caitlyn I'm here," she said.

"What?" Immy said. "Why not?"

But Riley had overheard their conversation. "They're not allowed to do anything without Caitlyn. Not even breathe."

"Don't be stupid," Erin told him and stomped off.

Immy remembered what had happened at swimming earlier in the day—how Erin had actually looked worried that Caitlyn might have heard her saying something nice to Immy. Her brow furrowed as she looked at Riley. "Ugh. What is it with them?"

"It's not just about the tree and the cottage, if that's what you're thinking," Riley told her.

"What do you mean?"

"The thing is, there was this other girl here last year. Her dad was working at the hospital as well, but they stayed just six months before they went back to New Zealand. As soon as this girl arrived, she and Erin became friends. And then Zara, too. Caitlyn was kind of left out. There are quite a few parents who don't like their kids hanging around Caitlyn. You know, because of the tree."

"Oh," Immy said. Things were starting to make sense as to why Caitlyn behaved the way she did. She was scared—scared not just of the tree but of losing her friends again. For some reason, Immy thought back to what Mrs. Garland had told her on her first visit to the library. Nothing is ever all good or all bad. Nothing is ever all black or all white. Suddenly she felt a bit sorry for Caitlyn. And for Erin, too. They were all stuck living in the shadow of the tree. The whole village was. Its blackened branches had crept into their lives in all sorts of ways.

"Hey, I forgot to give you this before." Riley pulled a torn-off piece of paper out of his pocket and pushed it at her. "It's my phone number. Call me if you want to go to the library Saturday afternoon."

Immy took the scrap of paper. "I don't know. . . . I've never done anything like that. Gone somewhere without telling my parents, I mean."

Riley just shrugged that shrug of his again, as if he didn't mind either way, and went back over to join the other boys.

* * *

After an embarrassing argument about whether she could walk herself home or not (Immy insisted that she could), Immy's dad left, and Mrs. Garland told them what they'd be doing that afternoon. They spent half an hour weeding and then set about picking glossy crimson-colored red currants, which Mrs. Garland said she'd make into red-currant jelly, promising them each a small jar.

Unfortunately, Mrs. Garland was busy, and Immy didn't get a chance to ask her any more about the tree. She told herself to be patient. She'd get a chance. She just had to give it time. Which wasn't exactly something she had a lot of, but still . . . She let it go for today. She'd seen how uncomfortable Mrs. Garland was when it came to talking about the tree. And Immy knew from experience that the more she asked, the less she'd probably find out. It was like when she bugged her mum and dad for something. The more she bugged, the less likely she was to get it. She just had to keep going to the library and come to the allotment club each week and hope Mrs. Garland might tell her more in time.

At just after five, Immy walked herself home. The wind was picking up and the sky darkening, and she wondered if it would rain this evening. As she let herself through the front gate, she heard something, and her eyebrows raised in surprise. Was that . . . ?

It was.

Immy rounded the corner of the house and stopped to watch her dad, busy with the whirring hedge trimmer. He was actually trimming the hedges.

And it looked like he'd gotten quite some way around the garden, too.

Immy waved, catching his attention, and he turned the hedge trimmer off.

"You needn't look so surprised." He lifted up his protective glasses, resting them on his head.

Immy was suddenly silent.

"Well, okay. I know it must be a shock to the system, but—Oh, come on," he said, taking in the growing horror on her face.

But it wasn't her dad's gardening efforts that Immy was reacting to. It was something else entirely.

Immy pushed her windblown hair out of her eyes, which were fixed on something by her dad's feet. Something small and brown that was shuffling across the grass.

Something small and brown and . . . bleeding.

17

Under the Hedge

Immy ran over and knelt down by the creature. It was about the size of her hand and had a small, brown, furry face and salt-and-pepper spines on its back.

"A hedgehog." Her father came down beside her.

"Dad, its head!"

The blood was coming from a deep cut in the hedgehog's head, above its eyes and just before its spines started.

"What are we going to do?" Immy's voice was panicked.

Beside her, there was a distinct lack of movement from her father.

But there *was* movement from above. The shadows

surrounding Immy darkened. Lengthened. She felt like the tree was looking on, wanting to know what was happening.

And then it found out.

Immy could have sworn the tree screamed a high-pitched scream in the wind as an unwieldy branch swooped down toward her.

Immy reached up and covered her head protectively. There was no time to be scared of the tree right now.

"DAD!" Immy yelled.

He didn't move.

Immy bent down closer to the hedgehog. It looked up at her with its tiny black eyes and quivering nose, which stretched out toward her.

The poor thing had to be in terrible pain.

She had to do something.

Her mum was at work and probably would be for hours yet. The hedgehog couldn't wait that long.

Looking around for help, Immy caught sight of the wooden gate that led to Jean's house.

Jean.

Jean's husband had been a vet. She said she'd assisted him. Surely she'd know what to do.

Immy got up and ran over to the spot where her father had left all the gardening tools and plucked out a pair of gardening gloves. She pulled them on, then raced back over and carefully, gently, scooped up the hedgehog and cradled it to her as she made her way across the garden.

"Oh, dear," Jean said, ushering Immy inside the glass conservatory attached to her pink thatched cottage. She peered down into Immy's hands. "The poor little thing."

"Dad was trimming the hedges and . . ." Immy gulped. She could feel the tears coming.

Jean sighed. "Silly me. I should have warned you. Those hedge trimmers . . . they're a terrible nuisance. Almost as bad as the bonfires. The hedgehogs hide during the day, you see. They're nocturnal, so people simply don't know they're there when they go to trim their hedges or light a bonfire. Hmmm . . . that's going to need stitches."

Jean moved over and dumped a basket of laundry

onto an armchair covered in a print of huge, full-blown roses. Then she came back and took the hedgehog carefully from Immy.

"Now, I know it's upsetting, but I'm going to need you to keep your head, Immy, if we're to help this poor creature. I tell you what we'll do. I'll go and get a hot-water bottle and put the hedgehog in the basket with it to keep warm. Then I'll call the nice young man who bought my husband's practice from him and see if he can pop by on his way home this evening. Jonathan his name is. Meanwhile, you have a very special task. You need to go back to where you first saw the hedgehog and start searching in the bottom of the hedge for a nest. I suspect there might be some babies there. Hoglets we call them."

"Really? Babies?" Immy's mouth fell open.

"There are usually four or five of them. If you find some, they'll need to be brought back here so we can care for them, too. Now, off you run, and see what you can find."

Immy did just that, bolting out the door and almost taking the little wooden gate off its hinges as she opened and shut it with a bang.

Her dad was hovering around the spot where she'd left him, looking like he wasn't quite sure what to do.

Above, the tree bristled in the breeze, its armlike branches scraping and groaning.

Immy ignored both of them and ran over to where her dad had left the hedge trimmer. She got down on her stomach, close to the hedge. Almost immediately she saw an area that had a small clearing with a lot of leaves and twigs behind it. She crawled over closer to it and opened the space up with her hands. Maneuvering herself closer still, she removed some leaves.

And then she saw them.

"Ohhh . . ." Immy breathed. "Hello."

There were three of them curled up together, each one about the size of a miniature cupcake. Carefully, she reached into the nest and picked them up, one at a time. They felt warm and prickly in her hand. She placed each one on the grass until she'd collected them all. Then she gently picked them up again and made her way to Jean's without giving her father, or the tree, a backward glance.

Back in Jean's conservatory, Jean was tucking

the mother hedgehog into the laundry basket with the hot-water bottle.

"Ah, there you are!" she said. "Find anything?"

"Three babies . . . I mean hoglets." Immy came over to peer into the laundry basket. "Is the mum okay?"

"It's hard to say—shock can be a funny thing—but I think she'll be all right. We just need to keep her warm. The babies, too. Now, let me have a look at these little chaps." Jean peered into Immy's hands. "Adorable. About three weeks old, I'd say." She picked each one up in turn and inspected it. "A girl, a girl, and a boy. Let's pop them in here." She reached down and picked up what looked like an oven mitt.

Immy must have looked taken aback when Jean started to put them inside the mitt, because Jean laughed. "Don't worry, I'm not going to put them in the oven! I know it seems strange, but the mitt really does keep them warm."

A knock on the conservatory door made Jean and Immy turn around.

It was her dad. He looked quite green.

He cleared his throat. "Ah, hello, I've just come to . . ." He trailed off.

Jean looked from one of them to the other in the

quiet that followed. "Why don't we all go into the kitchen and we'll put the kettle on while we wait for Jonathan, the vet, to turn up?"

Jean made two cups of tea and a hot chocolate for Immy while Immy's dad hovered around the table. The laundry basket with all the hedgehogs in it sat on top, and his eyes kept flicking toward it nervously.

Jean ferried the three mugs over to the table and then placed a hand on Immy's dad's shoulder. "Now, Andrew, be a dear and fetch a packet of cookies from the pantry. There should be a few varieties to choose from."

Immy's dad startled, as if he'd been awakened from a dream, but he headed off in the direction of the kitchen. Immy watched him go, barely believing her eyes. Over the years, she'd seen him help out in all kinds of situations. Once, they'd been at the shops, and a little boy had fallen over on an escalator in front of them and cut his leg quite badly. And another time, there had been a car accident down the road from their house. He'd helped with that, too.

And now he couldn't deal with a hedgehog with a cut on its head?

Jean pulled out a chair at the round, polished wooden table and sat down next to Immy. "I thought your father was a GP?" she said, her voice uncertain. "Or did I get that wrong and it's only your mother who's a doctor?"

Immy's eyes remained glued to the table. "He used to be a GP."

Jean didn't ask any more questions.

Jonathan arrived soon after and set about giving the mother hedgehog some local anesthetic and stitching up her wound. "I think she'll be all right. And, thankfully, the babies aren't too small. I've brought a couple of heating pads you can use and some food and syringes and so on. As you know, Jean, they'll need three- to four-hourly feeds for the next week or so."

"Oh!" Immy stood. "We'll do it, won't we, Dad? We can look after them."

Her dad looked at her blankly, as if he hadn't been listening to Jonathan at all. "Hmmm? What was that?"

There was a long pause, and then Jean reached

over and patted Immy's hand. "Best I take them, Immy. I don't sleep much anymore, and you need your rest for school. You can come and see them every day. You can do the afternoon feed, if you like!"

Staring at her father, her jaw clenched, Immy slowly sat down again. Before she could say anything, however, Jonathan's phone rang and he answered the call. After a few seconds, he held the phone to his chest.

"Sorry, I'm going to have to run. A Siamese having problems delivering her last kitten. You know how it is." He smiled at Jean.

"Oh, I do, I do. Thank you so much for dropping by, Jonathan. Very kind of you."

"Anytime. Er, not that I'm hoping you'll be injuring hedgehogs left, right, and center, of course! I'll show myself out!" Jonathan waved as he made his way to the front door. "Lovely to meet you, Andrew and Immy," he called out.

"Yes, you, too," her father managed to say, just a bit too late.

But Immy couldn't squeeze even a word out.

Her body was too busy dealing with the rage that was whirling around inside it.

18

Red-Hot Anger

Jean waited until she heard the front door open and shut before she checked her watch.

"Goodness me, look at the time. Your dad's probably got to get dinner on, Immy!"

Immy's dad checked the time as well. "Oh, yes. I should. Katie will be home soon."

"You head off. I'll just get Immy to help me set the hedgehogs up and then I'll send her on home."

"Of course . . ." Immy's dad was already backing out of the room toward the conservatory. "And I am sorry . . . about all the bother."

"It's no bother at all," Jean said. "Injured animals day and night. That was my life for decades!"

Immy's dad disappeared without another word.

As for Immy, she fixed her eyes upon the table and tried to remember to breathe. In and out. In and out.

"Oh, dear." Jean sat down beside her. "I can see you're angry, Immy, but some people simply aren't animal people, dear. It's just the way it is."

Immy's expression remained set. "It's not that."

"No?"

Immy's eyes met Jean's, and she realized she could tell her. She took a deep breath. "Something happened. In Australia. To one of his patients. It wasn't his fault, but it's why . . . why he isn't working anymore. Why he can't do *anything* anymore. Or doesn't want to, I mean."

"Ah, I see," Jean said.

There was something in her voice that made Immy look over at her.

"That happens sometimes, you know, with medical people. It's the same with vets. There are some patients who are different. Special. Who stay with you forever. I don't think it matters if they're people, or horses, or cats, or dogs. Maybe even hedgehogs. My husband once cared for a dog that was particularly special. It belonged to a woman in the village whose son was a soldier. It had been his dog, and when her son died, the dog was all she had left of him. The day my husband had to put the dog down, oh, it was awful. Just awful. It was no one's fault. It was just . . . life. But it was awful just the same, and he retreated inside himself for some time. I suppose what I'm trying to say is that sometimes people who care can care so much that it affects their own lives. Their own families. Do you understand?"

Immy nodded. But the truth was, she didn't understand. She didn't understand why her dad couldn't help with the hedgehogs because Bob had killed two people.

She didn't understand *at all.*

Immy tried to remain composed as she helped Jean with the heating pads, and then she left. She closed the conservatory door gently. The rain had started now, and the wind whipped around her. She zipped up her school sweater and walked as normally as she could to the little gate in case Jean was watching. The gate clicked shut behind her.

And then she ran.

Immy was as furious as the wind, which was battering the garden this way and that. She sprinted across the garden, heading straight for the French doors of Lavender Cottage.

She was almost at the doors when it happened—one of the tree's branches strained in the wind, bent down, and whipped her on its way back up again.

"Oh!" Immy grabbed at her arm, where the tree had clipped her. She stopped and, slowly, looked up.

The tree towered above her, its branches thrashing about violently. It looked almost as angry as she felt. Well, that meant that each was as angry as the other. "He didn't mean to do it," she yelled up at the tree. "It was an accident!"

The tree didn't listen. It continued to hurl its branches around above her, making Immy angrier still.

"It's all about you, isn't it? I don't know what your problem is, but other people have problems as well, you know. It's been . . . it's been hard for him. Not that you care!"

She took off then, bursting through the French doors, leaves flying everywhere.

Her father was in the kitchen, and it looked like her mother had just arrived home, because she was standing with her handbag still on her shoulder, the car keys in her hand.

Immy didn't even close the French doors behind her. Instead, she stood there, the wind hurtling past her into the house.

"You didn't even try!" Immy yelled at her dad. "You hurt the hedgehog, and you didn't even try to help her! A tiny little hedgehog. Bleeding! On our lawn. You cut her head open, and you just stood there. *What is wrong with you?*"

Both her parents stood stock-still.

When it became clear that neither of them had any idea what to say, Immy burst into tears. She ran past the table and bolted for her room. She made it halfway up the stairs before her parents moved into action, her father crossing the room in an instant.

"Come back here, young lady," he said to her, standing at the bottom of the stairs.

Immy stopped where she was on the stairs, her back to her father.

"What do you think you're doing?"

Immy turned. Her mother had followed and was hovering behind him, looking uncertain. She was still holding her bag and her keys. She looked like she'd love nothing more than to open the front door, get back in the car, and drive off. Probably back to work.

"You do not storm out of the room like that." Her father continued to lecture her. "That is not who you are."

Immy stared down at her dad with cold eyes. "How would you know?" she said. "How would you know who I am? You don't even know who *you* are anymore."

And then she ran the rest of the way to her room and slammed the thick wooden door behind her.

19

In the Stillness

The tree wailed and scratched at her window all night.

Immy finally fell asleep in the early hours of the morning. When she woke, her mum had already gone to work. Ignoring her dad as much as she could, she had a quick breakfast, then took herself off to Jean's to help out with feeding and caring for the hoglets and their mother. Immy loved feeding the hoglets. She picked each one up carefully—their little spines like a spiky toothbrush in her hand. Cradling them in a soft blanket, she then fed them their special milk in a syringe. They nibbled away on the end of the syringe hungrily. In that short time, she forgot what was going on at home. She forgot about her dad, who couldn't work. She forgot about her mum, who worked too much. And she forgot about the tree, which obviously hated her and was probably plotting to do something terrible to her on the eve of her birthday.

It was after she got home from Jean's on Saturday morning that she felt that the long afternoon was looming. She couldn't stop thinking about how the tree had lashed out at her last night.

And what it might do next.

She started to think about Riley's offer to go into town to the library. Immy got Riley's phone number on its scrunched-up piece of paper out of her desk drawer and held it in her hands. Her heart raced even considering making the trip. If her dad found out she'd done something like that . . . well, he'd absolutely lose it. But the more she thought about it, the more she shrugged her feelings of guilt away, telling herself that she wouldn't have to be so secretive if he had bothered to take her into the city when she'd asked. Once upon a time, her dad would have jumped at the chance to take her into Cambridge to the big library. This dad couldn't be bothered. He couldn't be bothered to do *anything ever.*

When she was sure her dad was busy in the kitchen making lunch, Immy made her way to the dining room table but no farther. Then she called out to him.

"Would it be okay if I went to my friend Riley's house this afternoon?" she asked casually. In reality, she had to pause to take a deep breath first because her heart was jumping around so much in her chest. "We, um, might hang out there a bit and on the village green as well."

Her dad's head appeared around the corner from the kitchen. "Riley that I met at your allotment club?"

Immy nodded.

"It's okay with his parents?"

"He asked me earlier this week, but I said I wasn't sure." Immy avoided the question.

"Well, I don't see why not. It's good you're making friends." His head disappeared again. "As long as you're back by five o'clock on the dot."

Immy gulped. "Can I call him to tell him I can come? He gave me their number." She looked at it, damp in her sweaty hand.

"Of course."

Immy picked up her dad's phone off the table and left the room. She took a seat on the stairs because her legs felt so shaky. She called Riley's number. His dad answered, and she asked if she could speak to Riley. Then, within seconds, there he was.

"Hello?" he said.

Immy couldn't speak.

"Hello?"

"It's me," she said. "Immy. I . . . that is . . . could we go?" Her voice dropped to a whisper. "This afternoon?"

"Sure." He didn't even hesitate, his voice breezy, as if she'd asked him for nothing more than to borrow a pencil at school. "How about we meet at two? There's a bus that comes ten minutes after that from just outside the village shop."

After eating her sandwich, Immy rushed up to her room, grabbed her backpack, and packed and re-packed it as if she were planning an expedition rather than a quick trip to the library. She ended up deciding on a notebook and two pencils and her purse, which had a fifty-pound note in it—a present from her parents to soften the blow of moving.

At two o'clock precisely, Immy went to say goodbye to her dad, who was reading a book in the living room.

"I'm going," she said. "He's in the yellow house, just up the road."

Her dad looked up over the top of his book. "And you'll be back at five o'clock?"

Immy nodded.

They stared at each other for a moment or two, so much unsaid between them.

Finally, her dad sighed. "All right. I'll see you at five."

Immy turned left out of the front gate and made her way up the street. She stopped at the village shop and watched as Riley exited his house. He waved to her cheerfully and then crossed at the crosswalk and met her at the bus stop.

"I can't believe how calm you look," Immy said. "Do you do this all the time?"

"Sneak off to the library?" Riley gave her a look. "No. Though my parents would probably be ecstatic if I did."

"You know what I mean. Anywhere."

"You seriously need to calm down. What do you think's going to happen? We'll get on the bus, we'll get off at the library, we'll find out stuff about the tree, we'll get back on the bus, we'll get off the bus back here. It's no big deal."

"You're braver than I am."

Riley laughed. "Hey, you're braver than, like, pretty much every single person in this village. No one else would have dared to live in that house. Look, here's the bus now."

Immy checked that the coast was still clear and that her dad was nowhere to be seen. She fumbled with her backpack while getting her purse out, then dropped it and picked it up off the ground. "Do we have to hail it or something?"

Riley stuck his arm out. "Yes. That's how they know to stop. Listen, you're not going to puke or something, are you?"

"No!"

The bus doors opened, and Riley went to get on. "I'll pay for us," Immy said. "I've got some money." She stepped in front of him and pulled out her fifty-pound note. The bus driver sighed when he saw the large note. Immy panicked. "It's all I've got!" she told him.

"Two children round-trip to St. Isles, please," Riley said, counting out the correct change.

Two tickets spat out of the machine, and the driver said nothing else about it.

"I'll pay you back," Immy said as Riley swung into a seat in the middle of the bus. She sat down next to him and put her head in her hands as the bus pulled away. "I'm never doing this again."

"You haven't even done it yet!" Riley burst out laughing. "Look, it'll be fine. After you called me, I called Mrs. Marsh at the library to tell her we were coming. Trust me, she is crazy overexcited. She'll probably have looked everything up by the time we get there, and we'll be back here within an hour."

20

At the Library

When the pair entered the small library, Riley immediately pointed out a woman behind the returns desk.

"That's Mrs. Marsh," he said.

Immy saw that she was busy talking to a man with a pile of books.

"We'll catch up with her later. Come over here," Riley said, beckoning her to follow.

He walked past a couple of large desks and then past an area with some armchairs to the other side of the library.

"These are the photos I was telling you about."

"Wow." Immy looked over the large wall, which

was covered with framed black-and-white photographs. Up on the top, painted on the wall, were the words ST. ISLES HISTORICAL SOCIETY. Immy stepped forward and began to inspect the photographs more closely. There was a group of three young women with long, straight skirts, high collars, and their hair piled loosely on top of their heads, which read TEACHERS, ST. ISLES INFANT'S SCHOOL, 1907. Next was another group, this time of men: returned soldiers of St. Isles celebrating Peace Day, 1919. Immy noticed that one of the men in the front row had only one arm. Next was a happier photo of a group of laughing women who looked like they were throwing small hoops over glass bottles. It read ST. ISLES CARNIVAL, 1926. Immy stared at the photographs in wonder. It was strange to think that these were once real people. People who'd wondered what clothes to wear that day, made plans with their friends, decided what to have for lunch at the carnival . . . all those everyday sorts of things.

The next photograph was a busy one. It was of a street filled with tables and bunting and flags instead of cars—a street party. "Oh, look!" Immy said when she read the label on the photograph. "It's VE Day in St. Isles—to celebrate the end of the war in Europe.

That's the day that Elizabeth disappeared," she told Riley as he came over.

He took a look. "I've found something, too," he said. "Over here."

Immy followed him over to inspect another photograph. "It's our street," he said. "And look—there's your place." He pointed to a house at the end of the street. "You can even see a bit of the tree."

Immy stepped in as close as possible to the grainy photograph. Riley was right. There was the village green, and up the street was Lavender Cottage and the black tip of the tree threatening the thatched roof.

They both stared at it.

"That tree could really do with some therapy," Riley finally said.

"Ah, here you are, Riley!" A voice came from behind them, making them both jump. "You must be Immy." The woman stuck her hand out. "I'm Susan Marsh."

Immy shook her hand and introduced herself.

"How interesting that you're living in Lavender Cottage. It has a long history, as I'm sure you're aware."

"I know a bit about it," Immy said. "I'd like to know more. People don't want to talk about it much."

Mrs. Marsh nodded. "Yes, well, it doesn't surprise me. Memories last a long time around these parts. I booked you in for some computer time. In fact, I hope you don't mind, but I couldn't stop myself from doing a bit of research for you after Riley called."

Riley threw Immy an "I told you so" look.

"Now, there's not a lot of information—barely anything on the first girl, Bridget, and only a little on the second. . . ." Mrs. Marsh paused.

"Elizabeth," Immy said.

"That's it! Thank you, it slipped my mind. Anyway, come and take a look at what I found. I've put all the newspaper articles up on two computers for you so you can read at the same time."

Immy and Riley sat at their computers and read as fast as they possibly could, stopping only now and then to point out to each other things of interest. While there were quite a few articles about Elizabeth's disappearance, they pretty much all said the same thing and came to the same conclusion: the police thought Elizabeth had run away. Being an evacuee from London, she was assumed to have simply run home. However, when she didn't turn up there within a week or so, they began to delve a little deeper, especially as she'd apparently not taken any of her belongings with her and was dressed only in a nightgown.

One longer article with the headline "Hemingford D'arcy Prowler?" claimed to have fresh news about the case. It talked about how, on the day she disappeared, Elizabeth had told a friend that she had seen something in the tree the day before. The police seized upon this information, and because there was no sign of a struggle in Elizabeth's room, they came to the swift conclusion that someone had persuaded her to run away with them. The article also made it quite clear that no one from the village believed that this was what had happened. Everyone quoted said they knew the truth: the tree had taken a second girl from the same family.

"One thing we know for sure," Riley said, as they finished up their reading.

"What?"

"No one in this village ever changes their mind about anything."

"What do you think Elizabeth saw in the tree?" Immy replied.

"Don't know. A person, I guess. Do *you* think she ran away?"

Immy wasn't sure how to answer, or how much to tell Riley. "Who runs away with nothing but their pajamas?"

"I think the police were right, and someone persuaded her to leave with them. They had clothes and stuff for her."

"Maybe," Immy said. But she didn't sound sure.

After they told Mrs. Marsh what they'd read, she gave them a few more photo albums that she'd dug out. They held mostly old photographs of their own village. The pair pored over these, Mrs. Marsh coming over to comment occasionally between her duties.

They'd just been looking at a bunch of old photos of the mill where Immy and her parents had viewed an apartment when Mrs. Marsh glanced at her watch. "Oh!" she said. "It's almost five o'clock. I should be closing up."

Immy's eyes shot to meet Riley's. "Five o'clock? Quick! We've got to go!"

Immy thanked Mrs. Marsh, and the pair raced for the library door.

"We need to cross at the crosswalk and catch the bus going back in the other direction," Riley told her. "It should be here in the next ten minutes."

They crossed the road and made their way to the bus stop that Riley had pointed out. As they waited, Immy bounced from foot to foot, her eyes trained on the traffic and the nonexistent bus.

"It's not coming!" Immy glanced back at Riley, who was sitting down.

"It's not supposed to be here yet," he said. "Five more minutes. Don't panic!"

But Immy was panicking.

She was panicking *a lot*. Finally, the bus came.

They were the first ones on, but they had to wait for everyone else to get on, too. Immy's legs jiggled up and down, impatient. "Come on!" she said, over and over again, under her breath.

Finally, they pulled away from the curb.

It took another fifteen minutes to get back to their

village, and by the time Immy caught sight of their street and Riley pushed the button so they could get off, it was five twenty.

She knew she was already in trouble. She just knew it.

As the bus pulled up at their stop and they stood waiting to get off, Immy saw her father. He was striding purposefully toward the village green.

"Look!" She grabbed Riley's arm. "He's headed for the village green. He's already been to your house. I can tell."

Riley spotted her dad and nodded. Then he glanced back at Immy. "Don't panic," he said. "I've got an idea."

Riley dragged Immy across the crosswalk and beckoned her inside the village shop, which was open until six.

"What are we doing in here?" Immy hissed at him.

"Quit asking questions and just get us two ice creams. Different ones."

Immy looked at him like he was crazy.

"Just do it already!"

Immy went over to the large ice-cream freezer bins with their sliding clear plastic doors and picked out two different ice creams. She took them back to Riley.

"Now pay for them, genius!" he told her.

Immy took them over to the man behind the counter and paid.

"Now what?" she said, making her way over to Riley, who was standing at the door. He took the ice creams from her and ripped the wrappings off both and handed her one.

"Now we stand outside your place."

It took about five minutes before her dad arrived back at Lavender Cottage. Immy felt so sick to her stomach that she'd barely taken a bite of her ice cream, which was melting all over her hand.

Her dad had just begun to open his mouth to let her have it when Riley stepped forward and cut in. "Sorry, Dr. Watts," he said. "I think I took too long choosing my ice cream, and I made Immy late."

Immy stared at Riley, her mouth open, her ice cream dripping on her toes. A decent excuse *and* remembering her father's proper title? Seriously, he was *so good* it was almost scary.

21

On and On

Immy's dad bought Riley's excuse, and the following week dragged on in much the same way as the weekend had started. Immy and her dad skirted around each other, talking about not much more than what cereal she wanted and whether she needed her PE uniform today. At first, Immy couldn't believe her luck. Not only had she gotten away with her trip to the library, but her parents hadn't punished her for being rude to her dad and slamming her bedroom door on them. She'd been sure she'd be grounded (not that there was anywhere much to go), or she'd be on dishwasher duty for a solid month. But as the days wore on, she began to feel less lucky. Instead, she started to feel awful about both the library trip and how her parents were ignoring the fight they'd had. She regretted what she'd said and didn't know what to do or say to make it right. So she did and said nothing at all.

Something else came back to her as well.

The rhyme.

The tree was angry with her, she just knew it. It had given her a warning—first the rhyme, then that strange shock. Immy had backed off, and it had calmed down. But the hedgehog incident had flamed the fire of its anger again. Maybe even her visit to the library, too. Maybe it knew about that as well?

It saw things. It knew things. Immy was sure of that much.

She started to hear the rhyme all the time. In the classroom, on the walk to school, in the library. At first she thought it was Caitlyn, hiding around corners, trying to get to her. But she soon realized it wasn't. Because she heard it other places as well. In the shower. At the supermarket. In bed.

Always in bed, with the tree's fingers screeching down the window's glass.

Do naught wrong by the mulberry tree,
or she'll take your daughters . . .

one,

two,

three.

In the dead of night, spirited away,
never to see an eleventh birthday.

She tried to close her mind to the rhyme and to the tree's endless scraping—to think of other things. As each hour passed, it became more and more difficult to push everything away. Just like it was becoming more and more difficult to pretend it was business as usual within their family.

Immy was at Jean's one evening after dinner. She'd just finished feeding the hoglets, and Jean was toileting them (something Immy didn't like doing). To do this, Jean stretched out each hoglet in turn in one hand and then rubbed it with a cotton swab dipped in sweet almond oil to make it go to the toilet. When each hoglet was done, she passed it to Immy.

"The vet's coming by this evening," Jean told her, after they'd worked in silence for a little while. "I think we might not need to do this for much longer.

The hoglets are putting on weight beautifully. They should be ready to feed and toilet themselves within the next few days, I think."

"Really?"

Jean nodded. "They've all done very well. *You've* done very well. You've taken such good care of them. You've listened carefully and learned a lot."

There was another stretch of silence.

"So." Jean finally glanced up from the last hoglet she was holding. "Everything all right at home?"

She asked the question in the casual way adults use when they think kids won't guess what they're doing.

Seeing Immy's look, she sighed. "Sorry, I'm not prying."

"It's okay," Immy replied, stroking the two hoglets in her hand. She wasn't sure what to say. But after what Jean had told her about her husband and the special dog, somehow she knew she'd understand. So Immy told her about Bob. She told her *everything.*

"Oh, Immy," Jean said when she was done. "That's terrible. A terrible thing to have happened."

Immy nodded, a lump in her throat.

"Your dad must be a very good GP if it's affected him this much. His patients must miss him." Jean passed her the final hoglet.

Immy shrugged.

"*You* must miss him."

She did, she realized. Her father was still here, yet he'd left at the same time. She missed him not just listening but also hearing her answers to the questions he asked her automatically when he picked her up from school. She missed their bike rides. She missed him swimming with her. She even missed their terrible attempts at baking. Yes, he was still here, but she missed him being *present*, which was something else entirely.

Immy concentrated very, very hard on the three hoglets she now held in in her hands, scared she was going to cry. She could feel Jean's eyes on her. She wanted to tell her so much. She wanted to tell her how she felt about the change in her dad. And about the rhyme. And about Caitlyn and school.

But she didn't.

Silence filled the room. It was some time before Jean spoke again, and when she did, her words were soft and quiet.

"Immy, do you see how carefully you're holding the hoglets? That's how you've got to hold your father's heart right now. And then, one day, I think you'll be surprised. I think that one day—hopefully soon—he'll be ready to forgive himself for the part he played in what happened, and the world will be there waiting for him. Does that make sense?"

Immy looked up now. She nodded again, even though she wasn't really sure if she believed Jean.

"I suppose there is one benefit to looking after your father rather than the hoglets." Jean's eyes twinkled.

"What's that?"

"You don't have to help him go to the toilet."

As soon as Immy walked through the French doors that evening, she knew something was up. Her parents were sitting at the table, and they looked like they'd been doing some serious talking.

This couldn't be a good thing.

"Take a seat," her mother said, her expression giving nothing away.

Reluctantly, Immy sat down at the table.

"I was just saying to your dad that maybe we should make plans for your birthday. I know we'd spoken about going to Paris, but work is being difficult about my taking time off so quickly. If you're worried about staying here the night before your birthday, we could go away somewhere close by?"

"No," Immy said quickly. "I don't want to go away." She wasn't sure if she meant this. She *really* didn't want to go away with her parents right now, but the alternative, staying here—did she really want to do that?

The rhyme started up in Immy's head again.

Do naught wrong by the mulberry tree . . .

She willed the words away as her mother kept talking.

"Anyway," her mother continued, "we can talk about it later, but I was thinking . . . maybe we could plan a little party. I know things didn't get off to the best start!"—she glanced at Immy's dad, and Immy realized he'd finally told her what had happened with the journalist and Caitlyn—"but maybe we could try to make amends. Your birthday's on a Sunday. It will be good timing. We can do something in the garden. It's a week and a half from today, so there's still time to send out some invitations."

The rhyme stopped in Immy's head as if it had hit a brick wall.

"What, you mean in the back garden?" she said. She could feel the tree through the French doors, behind her. She was sure its branches were creeping closer to listen in.

"Well, yes," her mother said.

Immy looked at her mother like she was insane. "Who would we invite?"

"Your whole class. Their parents."

She had to be joking.

"No one would come," Immy said flatly.

"It *is* a bit of a statement, Katie," Immy's dad said. "Apparently no one in the village will even walk in front of Lavender Cottage. And I told you how those women acted when we went to buy uniforms. I don't think they're going to forgive me so easily."

Immy was surprised to hear him say this. Finally, something they could agree on.

"If they came, it would only be to see whether I'd been taken in the night," Immy said, adding silently to herself *or she'll take your daughters . . . one, two, three.*

Immy's mum shrugged. "I thought it might be a good idea. A fresh start," she said. She sounded tired.

Well, Immy didn't care if she was tired. She was tired, too. Of Caitlyn. Of her father. Of her mother's work. "I thought this *was* our fresh start," she said.

Her parents' heads both snapped up.

And it was this one small comment that did it.

Everything simmering away in the family pot came to a boil.

22

Making the Best of Things

"Sorry, but I did think that!" Immy said. "I mean, how many fresh starts can one family have?"

"Immy!" her mother replied.

"Well, it's true!"

"You wanted to live in this house, Immy," her dad told her. "And I know things haven't gone exactly to plan, but we're trying to make the best of it. Your mother is trying to help you smooth things over with everyone by kindly offering to throw you a birthday party."

Immy was instantly sorry she'd stood up for her father the other night. She'd defended him to the tree. Now she forgot all about holding her father's heart carefully and stood from her seat. "I wanted to live here? No. I wanted to live in Sydney. With my friends. Near my school. That's where *I* wanted to live!"

Her dad slapped the table hard, making Immy jump. "Well, I'm sorry, but things change. People change. Not everything in life is always one hundred percent perfect. Just . . ." He ran a hand through his hair. "Just don't think that grown-ups have all the answers, Immy, because they don't. Sometimes they don't have any answers at all. Sometimes . . . sometimes they don't even know the questions."

He visibly deflated with each word, and as she saw this, so did Immy's anger. Suddenly she wasn't angry anymore. Instead, she was scared. Very, very scared. What if her dad never worked again? What if things were like this forever?

Her chin began to tremble. "You're a doctor! You're a doctor and you couldn't help the hedgehog. You hurt it and you couldn't help it."

"I know you don't understand . . ." her father said.

"Then explain it to me," Immy said, sinking back down into her seat at the table.

Her parents glanced at each other, and after a

moment, her mother nodded. When her father looked back at her, it was with shiny eyes. "A mother and her child died, Immy. I know it's been difficult for you to see that I played a part in that, but I did. And now a man just like me, with a wife and daughter just like me, has nothing. Nothing."

Immy's hands clenched under the table as she listened to her father. Didn't he think she knew this? Of course she did. They *all* understood this, and they all thought about that man every single day. What her dad didn't understand was something that had become obvious to her over the last few weeks. And now she saw she was going to have to spell it out for him, because it didn't look like he was going to work it out for himself. For someone with a bunch of degrees, he could be pretty clueless. Immy stared straight at him, unblinking. When she finally gathered her thoughts together and started speaking, her voice was measured. Controlled. "We know, Dad. We all know he's had everything he loved taken away from him. What I don't understand is how it will make things better for him *if you lose everything, too.*"

If she'd thought her father had looked beaten down before, the expression on his face now . . . As soon as she'd said the words, she wished she could take them back again. Swallow them right up. His back stiffened, and he pulled away from the table. He honestly looked like Immy had slapped him.

And then, in the silence, her mum's phone rang.

Everyone knew it was going to be work wanting her back in the hospital. It always was.

Immy couldn't bear to stay in the same room as them both another second longer. She stood from the table, her chair hitting the floor with a bang, narrowly missing the French doors. Then, just like the other night, she bolted from the room. She ran up the stairs into her room, slammed the door, and then pushed the desk in front of it. She didn't want to talk to either of her parents. She wanted to be alone.

Except she wasn't alone, of course.

Because she could hear it again. The rhyme.

Do naught wrong by the mulberry tree . . .

Immy crossed the room and flung back the curtains. Flipping open the lock, she pushed the window open wide.

And there was the tree, its spindly fingers reaching out toward her in the night. "What? What is it? What's your problem, anyway?" she said to its dark presence that saw the house cowering beneath it. "What have *you* got to be angry about? What's so terrible in your world that you have to steal girls away on their birthdays? You're just a tree! What problems could you possibly have?"

The moon behind it, the tree drew itself to its full height, its branches absolutely quivering with rage.

Before she could change her mind, Immy reached out as far as she could and did something she'd been too scared to do until now — she touched the tree. She grabbed at the closest branch. It was heavy and rough in her hand, and, immediately, a strong current of feeling coursed through her body. It was almost as if she were looking in a mirror, but it was her feelings that were being reflected back at her.

The tree.

It was just as angry as she was. She could feel it.

Immy could sense something else as well. Another feeling. A feeling that dragged her insides downward — sadness. The tree was sad.

With a gasp, Immy let go of the branch and staggered backward.

It couldn't be true. Trees didn't have feelings. What could a tree even want other than soil, sunlight, and water?

She stared at it, her mouth open, her eyes wide.

Or she'll take your daughters . . . one, two, three.

She took a step forward. "So? Are you going to tell me, then? What have you got to be angry about? Why are you sad?" But then she remembered what she'd just felt—that aching sadness. She tried her question again, in a completely different tone. "Can you . . . can you tell me what's wrong?"

In a split second, everything changed. There was a hush. All was quiet. The tree, the house, the village, time itself, held its breath.

Wanting to know more, Immy dared to take yet another step forward.

It was one step too far for the tree.

Without warning, a gust of air forced the window to bang hard in her face, and Immy stumbled backward, tripped over the rug, and fell to the floor with a *whump.*

She cried out, shocked, clambered to her feet in a moment, and pushed the window back open again. "I'm not scared of you," she yelled at the tree (she was, of course, but the tree didn't need to know that). "You're horrible. Horrible and mean. But I'm not scared of you. I'M NOT! I'm going to have that party on my birthday, *and* I'm going to put fairy lights in your branches. You'll see." She pulled the window closed again and locked it tightly.

It took another half hour or so before Immy's parents finally knocked on her bedroom door.

"I'm going to bed," she told them. "I'll talk to you tomorrow."

Her parents attempted to argue with her, somewhat feebly.

"I think we're all tired," her dad finally said to her mother. "We'll talk in the morning." After another minute or so, their footsteps retreated down the stairs once more.

Immy flicked her lamp off, put her pillow over her head, and willed herself to go to sleep.

23

Visitors and Visiting

At allotment club the following day, the group picked some beets, onions, and peas. Mrs. Garland had also brought them all some tiny white elderflowers to take home, from her mother's garden. She gave them all a recipe, too, for elderflower pancakes.

"That's what your mum used in the cake she gave us, isn't it?" Immy asked her. "Elderflower?"

"Oh, she made you the cake with the syrup? It's my favorite. Yes, you're right. The sugar syrup has elderflower in it."

A couple of the kids must have looked confused, because Mrs. Garland went on to explain. "My mother lives behind Immy. They even have a tiny little gate that joins up their gardens. They've been helping each other look after a family of hedgehogs after one was injured."

"Seriously?" Riley said.

Immy nodded. "They're really cute. There are three hoglets—those are the babies—and their mother. She was the one that was hurt. She's getting better, though."

"I've never seen a hedgehog."

"You can come and see them if you like," Immy offered. She looked around at the rest of the group. "You all can. It's good timing. My dad's picking up the hedgehog and her hoglets this afternoon. We're keeping them at our place because Jean—Mrs. Garland's mother—has to go to London to see a friend." When Jean had asked Immy's dad to look after the animals for the night, she could tell he was worried about doing so. That he still felt guilty about hurting the hedgehog and wasn't sure about caring for it.

A couple of the kids looked like they wanted to see the hedgehogs, but they knew that Immy's house was off-limits within the village.

"You've really got hoglets?" Erin asked.

"Yep. They're four weeks old," Immy said.

Mrs. Garland smiled. "They must be so sweet."

"I'll come." Riley grinned, giving the rest of the group a look that said he knew exactly why everyone else wouldn't. "I can stop by on the way home, if that's okay."

Mrs. Garland spoke up. "Actually, I have to fill my mother's bird feeder, so I might come, too, Immy, I'd love to have a peek. I haven't seen them yet."

"Sure," Immy said. "What about you, Erin?" It really seemed like she wanted to come.

Erin hesitated. "Um . . . I don't think so."

Immy shrugged.

"Well, then, let's pack up, and we can be on our way," Mrs. Garland told everyone. "I, for one, am desperate to hold a hoglet."

Mrs. Garland, Riley, and Immy walked the short distance to Immy's house together. Immy let them in via the front gate and walked them directly around the side of the house and into the back garden.

Immy glared up at the tree, trying to scare it into its best behavior.

"Wow, so this is the famous tree, huh?" Riley halted beside her.

"No, it's the one over there." Immy pointed to the very back of the garden, right near the little wooden gate, where the sickly-looking apple tree was still trying to make its escape.

"Hilarious," Riley said.

Mrs. Garland had crossed the garden and was standing closer to the mulberry tree. "Mum's still at it, I see." She gestured toward the white rose the tree had spat out of its bottom knot.

"Well, hello there." Immy's dad appeared from the French doors.

"Oh, hello, Andrew," Mrs. Garland said.

"Lovely to see you again, Claire. And Riley." He nodded at Riley.

"I know I told you I'm the librarian at Immy's school, but I'm also Jean's daughter. I hope you don't mind us barging in like this."

"Riley hasn't seen a hedgehog before," Immy explained. "So I said he should come and see them."

"And I *have* seen a hedgehog before, but I can't resist hoglets," Mrs. Garland added.

"Well, they're hard to resist," Immy's dad said. "Come and have a look. I've just finished feeding them, and they're having a bit of a race around."

"That's it," Riley said, getting up from the dining room table, which was covered in newspaper. He passed one of the hoglets back to Immy's dad. "I want a hedgehog. I want a whole room full of hedgehogs."

"Like a ball pit?" Immy laughed.

"Exactly! Even if it would be a bit prickly," Riley replied. "Hey, you know what? You should bring them to school."

"Oh, please, Dad?" Immy whirled around to look at her father, forgetting for a moment that this was the type of thing he didn't do anymore. Old Dad would have offered to bring the hedgehog and hoglets. Old Dad would have been pleased to do it. He would have told the kids all about what sort of care they needed, how to look out for them in their gardens, how to make their gardens hedgehog-friendly.

She wanted Old Dad back.

Immy turned back to the table. She wouldn't ask again.

And maybe her dad knew what she was thinking, because he spoke up quickly. "All right. I think I could do that. I don't have anything much on tomorrow."

Immy could barely believe it. "Really?" She looked up at him. "If you did, you could tell the kids all about what Jean's taught us. Taught me."

"It would be wonderful if you were able to," Mrs. Garland said. "Several of the other children wanted to come this afternoon . . ."

"But they were too scared." Immy's dad sighed, seeing where she was going.

Mrs. Garland nodded.

"Well, the hoglets are pretty active after eating. I could bring them in tomorrow after their mid-morning feed?"

"Immy's class has a library lesson just after first break, at a quarter to eleven. If you could make it in then, that would be perfect. I'll pull out a number of wildlife books and turn it into a little lesson."

* * *

At first break the following day, Immy gobbled her snack down and then headed straight for the library to help Mrs. Garland set up for her dad's visit.

"Is my dad here yet?" Immy said as she spotted Mrs. Garland in the corner of the library, shelving some books.

"Not yet." Mrs. Garland checked the clock on the wall. "Hmmm. . . . Do you think he'll be here soon? I put out some books and a few information sheets."

Immy's stomach sank. He should have been here by now.

Silently she walked over to the large glass window and stared outside toward the school gates.

"Immy?"

"He's not coming," Immy said. She wasn't angry. She wasn't shocked. She wasn't surprised. She was just . . . used to this now.

Mrs. Garland came over. "Do you think he's forgotten?" she asked.

"No." She didn't want to say any more, but she found that Mrs. Garland was like Jean. She had the same kind of face — she was the sort of person you could tell things to. "He's not . . . okay." She couldn't find the right words.

Mrs. Garland didn't say anything. Instead, she simply put a hand on Immy's shoulder. "I see. Well, maybe some other time. It's not a problem if he can't make it today. I haven't told anyone about the lesson."

Immy turned her attention back to the window.

And that was when she saw something.

24

A True Fresh Start

"I'll be back in a minute!" Immy told Mrs. Garland as she raced from the library. She sprinted down the corridor and outside into the playground. She rounded the corner of the building, heading for the school gates . . .

And stopped dead.

Caitlyn stood near the gates, looking out beyond them, at Immy's dad. Zara and Erin hovered behind, closer to the playground. Immy couldn't believe it. How had Caitlyn even spotted him? She was like the tree—she just seemed to *know* things. When Caitlyn heard Immy's footsteps, she turned. Immy was sure Caitlyn would say something nasty.

And she did.

"Your dad's out there," she said. "Being weird."

Immy's heart began to bang against her chest.

"Why is he even out there in the middle of the day?" Caitlyn's gaze moved to the other two girls. "Our real estate agent said he doesn't have a job."

Anger flared up inside Immy. She ran forward toward the gate. Caitlyn stepped sideways to block her way.

"What would you know?" Immy gave Caitlyn a shove with her elbow, pushing her aside. She opened the gate. "You don't know anything about my dad. He's a nicer person than you'll ever be. He . . . cares about things."

She didn't wait to hear Caitlyn's response.

She was too busy running toward the hedge that ran along the footpath and what she could see of her father's legs.

When she reached the hedge, Immy halted and crept up to peek around the corner. And there was her dad. Along with a cage with the hedgehog and hoglets in it that was sitting on the ground. It looked like he'd been pacing back and forth, because he was walking away from her.

Immy stepped out from behind the bushes.

"I thought you weren't coming," she said.

Her dad started and turned. "Me, too," he replied. "But I wanted to come. I wanted to come very much."

They stared at each other for a moment or two in silence, and then Immy broke into a run. She scooted around the cage and without slowing down, not even when she reached her father, hurtled herself into him with full force.

"I know," she said, her voice muffled by his shirt, which she began to wet with her tears. "I know you want to do all the things you can't do."

Immy's father kissed her on the top of her head and then sniffed, teary as well.

Some squeaking noises from down below made them both pull back. "I think they feel left out," Immy's dad said, staring down at the hedgehogs' cage.

Another squeak and then some snuffling.

"And that means they want to go inside," Immy said. "Come on, then." She took her father's hand. "I've been waiting for you."

* * *

"Oh, how lovely to see you, Andrew," Mrs. Garland said as Immy and her dad entered the library. "Thanks so much for coming in. I'll just finish grabbing a few more books and things. We've got about five more minutes before the bell rings."

"Over there." Immy directed her father to a table Mrs. Garland had set up, and they went over to place the cage on top of it.

Immy opened the cage and said hello to the hedgehog and her hoglets, who all continued to toddle around the cage, snuffling as they went. "I'm sorry," she said, glancing up at her dad. "For . . . everything. I know it's been hard."

Her dad reached out and smoothed her hair back. "It's been hard on all of us. But it won't be hard forever. I promise. I just need to find my feet. I am trying."

Immy nodded. "I know. I'll try harder, too."

"Thank you," he said, giving her a kiss on her forehead. "Now, listen. I think we should take the hedgehogs full-time. You were right about that. They should be my responsibility."

"Really?"

An excited, high-pitched squeak came from the

cage. "Do you think that means someone agrees?" he laughed.

A tiny nose exited the bars on the side of the cage.

"That girl," Immy said. "She's always hungry."

"She really is. You should have seen the way she scrambled when she saw the food coming this morning. I thought she might eat my fingers if I didn't hurry up! Can you tell them all apart?"

Immy nodded. "Of course! It's easy."

"I guess we won't be needing this, then." Immy's dad pulled three small bottles of nail polish out of his pocket.

"You're going to do their nails?"

Her dad grinned. "I thought they could use some pampering. No, Jean gave it to me. It's to put a little dot on their spines. If you use a different color on each one, you can tell who is who and then you can name them. You know, I think she might have been hoping we'd take them after this." He gave Immy a shrewd look. "She's smart, Jean."

"She is," Immy agreed.

"Why don't you name them now? Before everyone gets here?"

Immy bent down to peer inside the cage so she

could see all four hedgehogs at once. "Hmmm. Okay. Well, the other girl—the not-so-greedy one—she's the softest. And the sweetest." She paused to think for a moment. "Marshmallow?"

Her dad chuckled. "Sounds good. What about the greedy one?"

"Well, she really does always scramble for her food. Scramble?"

"Makes sense. And the boy?"

"He's dreamy. He needs a good poke to do anything. He always has his head in the clouds. So how about Cloud?"

"Marshmallow, Scramble, and Cloud. I like it." Her dad nodded decisively. "We've forgotten the mother."

Immy grinned. "How about Lucky?"

"Lucky it wasn't worse, you mean."

"Something like that."

"Lucky it is, then. Jean said they should be able to eat by themselves in just a few more days. Depending on how the mother heals, they might need to be kept over the winter, though. The vet is going to bring around a special, larger cage tomorrow."

Immy put a finger through the bars and tickled

Scramble on her tummy. "Can we keep them? Really? Until they're ready to be released?"

Her dad nodded.

And Immy stood up and hugged him right up until the library door opened and the students started to pour in.

25

Balancing on Logs

Immy's class separated into small groups, and each group took its turn gathering around the cage.

"Now, we're not all going to hold the hoglets, because that wouldn't be good for them," Mrs. Garland told each group. "But you can have a close look, and we'll all be learning lots about them and how we can care for them in our own gardens. I have a number of books that you might like to borrow and information sheets as well."

Immy's dad told the class all about how the hedgehog had been injured, how Jean had taken it and the hoglets in, what the hedgehogs needed on a daily basis, and how they'd be set free once they weighed enough and the season was right. He also told everyone how they could make their gardens hedgehog-friendly and said that they should watch out for hedgehogs in their sheds and hedges and check in bonfires before they were lit.

Immy couldn't have been prouder of him. It really was like having Old Dad back again, though she knew she shouldn't let herself get too excited. Coming to the school today had been hard for her dad. So hard, he'd almost not been able to do it. He'd been able to come inside only because she'd gone out and met him halfway. Immy remembered how Jean had told her she needed to hold her father's heart carefully, but Immy thought it was a bit different from that. It was more like her dad was balancing—balancing on top of a log, with his arms out, trying to keep steady. She had to hold his hand and help him get to the other side. She knew from experience that the funny thing about balancing on logs was that most of the time you didn't even need that hand. It was enough to know it was there. Just in case.

When the lesson was almost over and all the kids had wandered off to check out their books, Erin remained, hovering by the cage.

"Did the mother hedgehog's injury need to be stitched up?" she asked Immy's dad.

He nodded. "It did."

Erin bent down to take another look at the hoglets. "It's what I want to do when I'm finished with school," she said. "I want to be a small-animals vet."

Caitlyn was sitting at a table nearby, an information sheet in her hand that she obviously wasn't reading. "Well, you'd have to be good at biology," she said. "You know, growing things and everything. Maybe you should join the allotment club?"

Looks flew between the three girls. It was obvious that Caitlyn knew Erin had been going to the allotment club. Immy shrugged, letting Erin know she hadn't told on her. She was going to let it slide but then realized she was sick of Caitlyn. She was tired of being pushed around. Over her moods.

Immy spoke up. "You *should* join, Erin. It's great. Everyone there is *really nice. Really friendly.* It's nice to hang out in the sun with really nice, really friendly people."

Immy's dad watched the girls carefully, sensing that something was going on. "Well, um, that's good," he said. "And, yes, you do need to be good at biology to be a vet. But the thing is, it's easier to be good at something when you have an interest in it. Now, Erin, isn't it?"

Erin nodded.

"I think if we're very quiet about it, it might be fine for you to hold a hoglet or two."

After lunch, Immy took herself off to the library and settled down in one of the large beanbags with the book she'd almost finished reading. She was up to an exciting part, so when the library door opened and closed, she didn't look up.

Sometime later, there was a *whump* as someone sat down in one of the other beanbags. Again, Immy's eyes didn't leave her book — she had only a couple of pages to go now and wanted to finish the story before the bell went.

When she was finally done, she glanced to her left.

She could barely believe her eyes.

Because there, on the other beanbag, was Erin, reading.

Immy had been about to get up to find a new book, but now she decided against this. Instead, she sat very, very still, thinking that any sudden movement might scare Erin away.

After some time, Erin turned to her. "Your dad's really nice, isn't he?" she said.

Immy wasn't sure how to reply. "Yeah," she said. "Yeah, he is."

Erin went back to her book then, so Immy brought her own book back up to her face and pretended to keep reading.

26

In the Middle of the Night

"And that, my girl, is the last feed of the night done." Immy's dad steered her out of the living room, his hands on her shoulders.

"Good night, Marshmallow, Scramble, Cloud, Lucky," she called out as she went.

When they reached the top of the stairs, her dad waved her off into her room. "Let's all try to get a few hours' sleep before the next feed."

Immy yawned and padded her way into her room.

Today had been . . . interesting. Her dad turning up at school just when she thought there was no hope of him showing at all. Her finally standing up to Caitlyn. And Erin joining her in the library at lunchtime.

Sometimes change could be good.

Pondering this, Immy walked over to the bedroom window. Nervously, she opened the lock and pushed the window open.

There was the tree, as cheerless, surly, and bleak-looking as ever.

Immy considered it for a moment.

She'd changed her approach today and won.

Maybe she needed a different approach with the tree, too?

Immy went over and took the chair from her desk. She brought it to the open window and then sat there for some time, hugging her knees up to her chest in the cool of the evening. As she sat, she studied the tree carefully, its inky branches shadowy and somber against the sky.

Yes, a different approach had worked today. With her dad. With Caitlyn and with Erin.

She saw now that being angry with her dad had been a complete waste of time. She'd been so angry at him for so long that there'd been no room in her head to see his point of view — to see that he *wanted* to do all those Old Dad things but just *couldn't* do them. She'd tried to bully him into doing things. Making him feel even worse about himself. She'd hated Bob for this new life he'd given them all.

Hate and anger simply hadn't worked for her. Maybe this was where the village was going wrong with the tree? Their hate for the tree was obvious — so obvious that the tree carried the marks of hate on its skin. And the tree hated them back. Immy thought the tree's hate had leached into the villagers. Made bitterness brew in those who lived closest to it — like Caitlyn and her parents. But what if . . . what if they were all wrong? What if the tree didn't need to be cut down or defeated? What if . . .

What if what it really needed was to be understood?

It's what her dad had needed. Maybe the tree simply needed her to meet it halfway as well? Maybe then it would share its secrets with her — tell her why it was angry. Maybe then she'd truly know what had happened to those girls and she'd be able to keep herself safe.

Immy stood and opened the window wider.

"Hello, tree," she said, after a moment or two. "I

think we got off to a bad start. I'd like . . . well, I'd like to be friends. I'm sorry I yelled at you. I'm sorry I was rude."

Just like on the night before, everything stilled.

Except, this time . . . this time it felt like the tree wasn't going to slam the window in her face. This time it felt like it was really listening.

Immy cleared her throat. "I know you have problems, too. We all do. Anyway, I wanted to let you know that I'm here if you need me. I could help you with your problems if you like."

There was a long silence after that, the tree unstirring in the deathly quiet.

Eventually, Immy decided to leave things at that. She didn't want to scare the tree off. It would need time to think about her offer. To know that it was genuine.

So she went to bed.

For the first time, she left the window open.

27
A Good Day

Friday was a good day. Caitlyn was away from school, and Immy couldn't have been happier. It was like a dark cloud that had been hovering over the classroom had been blown away by a fresh breeze. People talked to her at lunch. Swimming was fun. After allotment club, Immy and Erin stood around and chatted for a while. Feeling bold, Immy asked again if Erin would like to come over. She was surprised when Erin agreed. Not too long ago Erin would have crossed the road to avoid walking past Lavender Cottage. What had made her change her mind? Had seeing the tree made her realize it wasn't as scary as the village made it out to be? Immy decided not to ask any questions in case Erin second-guessed herself. The girls walked back quickly to Immy's house, where her dad made them a snack while they fed the hoglets.

After Erin left, Immy closed the door behind her and turned to her dad. "Maybe we should have that party after all?" she said to him.

His eyebrows shot up in surprise. "Hmmm. . . . You think it's a good idea?"

Immy shrugged.

"Is it too late to send out invitations? We could make them over the weekend, but you'd have to give most of them out at school on Monday, and that would be less than a week until the actual party on the Sunday."

"If they want to come, they'll come."

Her dad inspected her for a moment. "You're sure you don't want to go away?"

"I'm sure," Immy answered quickly. "I want to stay. I want to be . . . strong."

"Strong?"

Immy nodded.

"Well, okay, then. I guess we can do that. Together. Come on, then. You start a list while I make dinner."

* * *

Immy and her dad went to an office supplies shop on Saturday morning. After her mother got home from her hospital rounds, the three of them spent the rest of the day making the invitations for the party. By Saturday night they were ready to be given out.

"Maybe I could give Jean's invitation to her tomorrow?" Immy said as they were getting ready for bed.

"Remember the lovely cake she made us?" Immy's mum said, dental floss in hand. "You should bake her something and take it around with the invitation. It would be a nice gesture."

Immy and her dad looked at each other dubiously. Like they'd told Jean, they'd tried baking before. Things rarely went well. Immy particularly remembered the cupcakes they'd forgotten about, which had turned black on the bottom. The top half had been edible, though. Sort of.

After breakfast on Sunday morning, Immy's mum went off for another round at the hospital, and Immy and her dad found a recipe for some raisin-and-oatmeal cookies. They turned out . . . okay. The problem was, some of the raisins sticking out on top of the cookies were a bit burnt.

"We should consider opening a charcoal restaurant," her dad said, eyeing the cookies. "I suspect we'd be very successful."

Immy inspected the cookies as well. "Do you think I should take them?"

"Maybe the less burnt ones."

"Are there any?"

"At least four. I'm sure of it."

While the cookies cooled, Immy helped her dad feed the hoglets. Then she put a selection of the less burnt cookies into a plastic container, found Jean's invitation, and told her dad she was going over there.

Immy knocked on the conservatory door and waited until Jean arrived.

"Hello, Immy!" Jean said, obviously pleased to see her. She paused to smooth her white hair. "I'm a bit of a mess, I'm afraid. I've been conquering the housework this morning."

"I just came over to give you this. Well, two things, really," Immy said, handing over the container and the invitation, on top of it.

"Two things! My, aren't I lucky! Well, I'll tell

you what. I was just about to make a cup of tea, so why don't you come in for a minute and have a hot chocolate with me to keep me company?"

"Okay," Immy said, though her stomach was jumping around a bit at what Jean would say about the invitation — what she'd think about them having a party in their back garden and about the fact that they weren't going away.

Jean puttered around, making the tea, and Immy helped fetch the hot-chocolate powder, sugar, and milk and some little plates. They sat down at the table and Jean opened the plastic container.

"Now, what do we have here?" She took a cookie out.

"It's all right, you don't have to actually eat them," Immy told her. "I'll just tell dad you did."

Jean laughed. "You really don't do much baking at home?"

"No. We prefer edible food."

Jean took a bite of the cookie and chewed thoughtfully. "Oh, come on, now," she said after she'd swallowed. "They're not bad at all."

Immy gave her a look.

She waved a hand. "They're really not. Next time, just set the timer for ten minutes and watch them from then on. Ovens are all different, you know. Do you have a thermometer inside the oven? It helps."

"Okay. Thanks for the tip. I'll get one for dad for Christmas. He needs it."

Jean laughed. "You are terrible. And how is he? I was so glad he took the hedgehogs. It made me very happy indeed."

"Things are better," Immy said quietly. "Better than before."

"I'm pleased to hear that." Jean smiled. "Now, what's my second thing?" She picked up the invitation and opened it.

She began to read it, and her brow creased.

Immy's stomach churned again.

Jean put the invitation down, her hands making the paper shake lightly. Their eyes met.

"You're not going to Paris?" Jean asked.

"No," Immy said. "Mum couldn't get the time off work."

The room was quiet.

"I know you're worried," Immy said hurriedly,

wanting to fill the silence. "About what could happen. The night before my birthday, I mean. But it will be all right, you'll see."

Jean studied her. "How do you know?"

"I just . . . know." She didn't. Not at all. But she knew it would be wrong to run away. To think only about herself and the fact that she was scared. She needed to know the truth about the tree. The village needed to know, too. Especially Jean. "You will come? To the party?"

"Nothing would give me greater joy than to come to your eleventh birthday party, Immy." Jean's words were loaded with meaning.

Immy knew what she meant. The party would be on her actual birthday. If she was there at the party, then everything was all right. She hadn't been taken.

They sat quietly for a moment or two, Immy staring at the untouched cookie on her plate.

"I have to tell you something," Jean finally said.

Immy looked up. "What's that?"

Jean's expression was dead serious. "It's about Elizabeth. In the days before she disappeared, she said she saw something. In the tree. That was all she said, and when I questioned her about it, she wouldn't tell me anything more. She said she was being silly, that she was seeing things and was sorry she mentioned it. I've always wondered . . ."

Immy sat forward on her chair. "Did you tell the police?" She asked the question even though she knew that Jean had. She remembered that someone had told the police that Elizabeth had seen something in the tree, and that someone was obviously Jean. This was why the police had thought Elizabeth had run away.

"Oh, yes, of course I told them. I was sorry I did in the end, because it was when they gave up on her, really. They decided she'd simply run off. They figured it had been a person she'd seen. That someone had been climbing up to her window. Someone she knew. And they thought this person had persuaded her to leave with them. But . . ."

"What?" Immy urged Jean on.

"Well, I don't think it was a person."

"What do you think it was?" Immy said, her heart racing. "What do you think she saw?"

Jean stared into the distance, frowning. "I . . . I don't know. Maybe something . . . magical. I know it sounds silly, I know it does. But that knot appearing overnight. Oh, it was very strange." She put a fluttery hand to her chest.

"Elizabeth didn't say . . . well, she didn't say she *heard* anything as well, did she?"

Jean snapped to attention, her eyes focusing in hard on Immy. "Why would you say that?"

Immy pulled back in her chair. "I . . . I don't know. I just thought maybe if she'd seen something, she'd also heard something."

"You're sure that's all you meant?"

Immy nodded. She wasn't lying. Not really.

Jean's eyes remained on her for what felt like a long, long time. It felt like forever before she spoke again. "One of the last things Elizabeth told me about the tree was that she'd heard the rhyme. You know the one—about the tree. She said she'd been hearing it in her head. As in, when no one else was around. The police didn't know what to say when I told them. Anyway, when I woke up one morning with the rhyme in my head, I was so scared. And then I got angry. I went straight out and yelled at the tree. I kicked it and I punched it and I told it I hated it. I told it I wouldn't be paying any attention to it—to things in its branches, or rhymes. I told it I'd never forget it had taken my friend. That I'd never forgive it and would come every day and leave a flower for Elizabeth. That I wouldn't forget her. Strangely, after I said my piece, it never bothered me again. Maybe because I was as angry as it was. Oh, I don't know what to believe about the tree. I never have. I only know it had everything to do with my best friend's disappearance. Everything. So please, Immy, if you see or hear *anything*, tell me. And do be careful as your birthday approaches. We can't have you disappearing, too."

28

A Visitor in the Night

On Monday, Immy gave out her party invitations at school. She left one on everyone's desk in the classroom and gave one to her teacher. She kept Mrs. Garland's invitation in her pencil case and waited until lunchtime and her usual library visit to give it to her.

Except when she got to the library, another teacher was there. Apparently it was Mrs. Garland's turn to do playground duty. After she'd been told this was the case, Immy stood at the library door and thought. She didn't want to go out to the playground, but the invitations really needed to be handed out today. She would have to do it. And by herself, too. She couldn't even ask Erin to come with her, because Erin's mum had picked her up early from school today for a piano exam.

Immy pushed open the library door, crossed the short expanse of hallway, and scanned the playground through the nearest window.

Mrs. Garland was at the edge of the asphalt playground.

And Caitlyn was nowhere to be seen.

Immy took her chance and ran out.

"Ah," Mrs. Garland said after reading the invitation. "Yes, Mum told me about your party."

Immy watched her expression carefully to see what she thought.

"I'd love to come, Immy. I'll let your mother know I can make it."

"Great!" Immy breathed a sigh of relief. Still not having had a chance to speak to Mrs. Garland about the one thing she was desperate to know more about, she took this as her cue to ask one more time for information. "Is there . . . is there anything else you can tell me about the tree?" Jean's words had spooked her slightly. If there was anything else anyone could tell her, she needed to know.

Now.

Mrs. Garland's gaze had been skating over the playground, but it came down sharply upon Immy now. "I'm sorry," she said quickly, "I really shouldn't have spoken to you about the tree at all. The staff has decided it's not something we want to encourage the students to discuss."

"Oh," Immy said. "Okay."

Mrs. Garland smiled. "That said, I think it's a great idea that you're having a party. Hopefully it will put all the silly rumors to rest." A screech came from the monkey bars. "Oh, dear. I'd best run and find out what's going on over there. Excuse me." And with that, she'd hurried off.

It was only then that Immy saw Caitlyn standing close by. She'd sneaked up from behind and had obviously heard the whole conversation.

Saying nothing, Immy turned and started in the direction of the library. Caitlyn ran over, cutting her off.

"What now?" Immy said, every muscle in her body tensing.

When Caitlyn didn't reply, Immy finally found the courage to look at her properly. She seemed to be struggling to say something. As if she wanted to but couldn't find the words, or something was stopping her. If anything, she looked scared rather than angry. Immy noticed something else as well. Caitlyn's eyes—they were different. They looked lighter. They'd been so dark before, and now they were definitely lighter.

Caitlyn's mouth opened yet again. She whispered something. At first, Immy thought she'd said the words *I'm sorry,* but that couldn't be right.

"What did you say?" she asked.

Her words broke the spell. Caitlyn shook her head. And then she turned and ran from the playground.

Immy watched her go. What was going on? This place—it was so strange; so full of secrets. So many things didn't add up. Didn't make sense. She thought that by now she'd have found out lots about the mulberry tree. About Bridget. About Elizabeth. About what had happened to them. Now she saw that no one was going to be able to tell her the truth about what happened to those girls.

Because they didn't know.

No one knew.

No one except the mulberry tree.

Only the tree had seen what happened on both those nights. Only the tree knew the truth.

Immy went straight to the tree as soon as she got home from school and was shocked by what she saw. She hadn't paid too much attention to the tree over the past few days — she'd been busy planning her party. But now she saw that it had changed. It looked droopy. Shrunken and unwell. She put both hands out without hesitation to hold on to the trunk and gazed into the bleakness above. She wasn't surprised that she didn't feel the pulsing of anger that she'd felt before. The tree simply didn't look up to it. Instead, the tree seemed tired. Tired and weak and sad. Always sad.

Immy also couldn't help but notice that one of Jean's roses was still wedged into the bottom knot, even though it was late in the afternoon. The tree didn't even have the energy to spit it out like it usually did.

What was going on?

As Immy inspected the tree's branches, she

remembered Jean's words and wondered what it was that Elizabeth had seen. Was it a person after all? Had someone persuaded her to run away?

"What happened to those girls?" Immy asked the tree. "Did you see? Do you know? You have to tell me." Her eyes moved downward to the tree's trunk and came to rest on the vicious marks that she and her dad had noticed weeks ago. She wondered if anyone had actually asked the tree what had happened before. Or had they simply come after it with axes and hate? "You can trust me," she told the tree. "I won't hurt you. I promise."

But the tree only continued to droop and offered up no answers.

That evening, Immy's mum had gotten home early, and they were about to have dinner. Immy was setting the table when there was a knock on the front door.

She went and opened it.

She almost dropped the cutlery in her hand when she saw who was standing outside—Caitlyn's mother. Immy had been right that day when she'd gone to get her uniforms. It had been Caitlyn's mother who'd been gossiping with the two other women. She and Caitlyn had the same dark hair. The same deep brown eyes. Caitlyn's mother walked her daughter to school each day, and Immy was very careful to avoid them both.

"Go and fetch your mother, Imogen," Caitlyn's mother said, her arms crossed.

Immy turned and ran into the kitchen.

"Who is it?" Immy's mum asked, inspecting the pasta sauce on the stove.

"It's Caitlyn's mother."

"Who?" Her mother looked over.

"Caitlyn's mother. Who owns the house."

"Really? What's she doing here? Legally they're not entitled to . . ."

Immy didn't care what was, or wasn't, legal. "It's about the party. It's got to be. Caitlyn's in my class, remember?"

Her mother finally put everything together. "Oh . . ." She started toward the front door, Immy in her wake.

"Hello." She held out a hand when she got there,

offering to shake Caitlyn's mother's hand. "Katie Watts."

Caitlyn's mother didn't uncross her arms.

After a second or two, Immy's mother dropped her hand with a sigh. "And how can we help you this evening?"

"I was hoping you could explain this." Caitlyn's mother held up Immy's crumpled party invitation.

"It's a party invitation," Immy's mother said.

Caitlyn's mother drew herself up to her full height. "Exactly. I knew I shouldn't have leased the cottage to outsiders. You've done nothing but make fun of our situation since you arrived here. Do you think the tree is a joke? Something to be laughed at? Thrown in our faces? Two girls disappeared. Do you know what that means to this village?"

"I think what happened to those two girls is awful," Immy's mother answered calmly. "An awful thing to have happened to their families, to the village. But I also think the tree is simply a tree."

"You shouldn't be having a party in that garden!" Her words were angry, but there was something else in her voice. Something a bit . . . frantic. She was scared, Immy realized.

"Perhaps if you could look at it in a different way," Immy's mum said. "Getting everyone together—it could be quite healing."

"No. No, I don't think so."

"Immy isn't even related to the other girls! Look, I know this . . . curse has been hanging over the village for generations, but maybe for a moment you could entertain the thought that it's not true. I'm hoping the party will put all the rumors to rest. It would be good for the village if it did."

"You're throwing the situation in our faces! You have no idea how this has affected my daughter. She's behaving very strangely. She's not herself these past few days. Something's wrong."

Immy frowned. Caitlyn had been away from school on Friday, and then, in the playground today, she'd definitely been behaving strangely. She remembered her lighter eyes. The words she couldn't seem to get out. And was it her imagination, or did Caitlyn's mother look a bit different, too?

"I'm sorry you feel this way," Immy's mother replied. "You're quite welcome to come along on the day if you change your mind."

Caitlyn's mother lifted her chin. "We will not be

changing our minds, and we will not be coming. In case you haven't realized it yet, no one else will be either."

"Actually, I've already had a number of people text us to say they will. But if you won't, all the more cake for us, I say. Good night!" And, with that, Immy's mother shut the door on their visitor. She immediately turned and looked down at Immy. "Goodness, talk about sour. Living with the tree for so long has done it to her, I expect. It's given the whole family black little hearts!"

Interesting, Immy thought. That was her theory, too. "Who said they'd come to the party?" she asked.

"Well, Jean and Jean's daughter for a start. Riley and his parents."

"Who else?"

Her mother looked sheepish. "That's it so far. I hope you're hungry for cake."

29
Changes

By lunchtime at school on Tuesday, all the kids were talking about the party—even the ones not in Immy's class. Several of them gave her weird looks, and Immy made sure to keep well out of Caitlyn's way. As she ate her lunch, Immy wondered what would happen over the next four days. Would others say something to them? Would the guests decide to come? Or would they stay away?

She was almost done with her lunch when Erin came and sat down beside her, placing her tray on the table.

"Oh," Immy said, surprised. "Hello." And she *was* surprised. Because while Erin had been coming to the library every day, they hadn't yet sat beside each other at lunch. Immy had never said anything about this, because she knew why — Erin was scared of what Caitlyn would say. Or do.

"You going to the library after?" Erin asked after a little while.

Of course she was. Where else was there for her to go? "Yes," Immy said. "You?"

"Why not," Erin replied.

Immy could think of a million reasons why not, but she didn't mention any of them to Erin.

Immy and Erin had both settled in on their respective beanbags in the library and were reading when Immy realized this was it. Erin had really taken a stand now. She wasn't just hiding out with Immy in the library. She'd had lunch with her, too.

They were officially friends.

Immy's head thought this was great. Her stomach, however, wasn't so sure. It churned, sensing the fight that was sure to come with Caitlyn.

The two girls hadn't been in the library for long

when the library doors were pushed open, making Immy glance up.

It was Caitlyn.

Watching her, Immy sat up in her beanbag. As soon as she saw her, she remembered the exchange in the playground. And Caitlyn's mother's visit to their house. There really was something . . . different about Caitlyn. She sensed it instantly. It wasn't just how she looked. It was her attitude as well. The way she let the door close limply behind her. The way she looked wary as she glanced around the library. The Caitlyn of before would have stormed in here. Demanded that Erin come outside with her.

Immy rose from her beanbag. Despite every bone in her body telling her not to, she approached Caitlyn.

She looked her in the eyes.

And she couldn't believe what she saw.

Caitlyn's eyes — they were lighter still. Her hair was lighter, too. It now had a reddish tinge to it.

Something about the change made Immy shiver.

The two girls stared at each other. As they did so, Immy was reminded of the tree. Of how it was fading. Sick and drooping.

"I don't feel well" was all Caitlyn said. "I feel so strange."

Mrs. Garland must have been watching them, because she approached at this point. "Caitlyn, are you all right? Are you not feeling well again?" she said. "I might call your parents."

Before Immy could say anything at all, Mrs. Garland had shepherded Caitlyn out of the library.

Immy returned to her beanbag, where Erin was looking on, curious.

"Caitlyn's been acting weird. It's almost like she's a different person. What was all that about?" Erin asked.

Immy continued staring at the spot where Caitlyn had been standing. "I don't really know," she replied.

But, somehow, she suspected she was about to find out.

Caitlyn didn't come to school the following day. Mrs. Garland told Immy that Caitlyn had a virus.

Immy didn't know what to believe.

When Immy walked home from allotment club

on Wednesday afternoon, she was surprised to find her dad in the back garden, cleaning off a large wooden table and eight chairs under the still-sickly mulberry tree.

"Where did that come from?" she asked.

"The little noticeboard at the supermarket," he said. "Someone was selling it, and I thought it might be useful for the party. They had a trailer, so they were even willing to drop it off. So, do you think a party will cheer the tree up? It looks like it needs it."

The pair turned to inspect the tree.

"Or maybe it's not the partying kind," her dad continued.

"Maybe not." If only she could figure the tree out.

"Oh, well. That wasn't my only good idea. Look . . ." He nodded farther into the garden, and Immy saw that the wooden playpen, which had been in the shed, was now set up on the grass.

Immy went over to take a closer look. "Oh, wow, they'll love this!" she said, realizing what her dad had done. He'd run some thick, clear plastic around the bottom half of the playpen, and the hoglets were romping about, having obviously just been fed while their mother slept the day away.

"They seem to like it."

Immy grinned as she pretended to watch the hedgehogs, but really it was her dad she watched, out of the corner of her eye.

She realized that it felt like ages since she had checked to see if he was taking his pills.

30

A Sighting

It was strangely hot on Thursday afternoon, and Immy and Erin were sprawled out on the table and chairs in the back garden. They were supposed to be doing their homework but really were mostly eating cookies (thankfully ones out of a package, which Immy's dad hadn't made). Immy hadn't had the courage to quiz Erin on her change of mind about visiting Lavender Cottage the last time she'd come over. But now she asked. Erin confided that her mother had encouraged her to spend more time with Immy. She said her mother had never really gotten along with either Caitlyn or her family and she didn't like all the village talk about the tree. She was pleased that Erin was making new friends.

Caitlyn had remained away from school, which made Immy nervous. She wasn't sure what to think about the change in her — in her eyes, her hair, her personality. She wanted to go and see Caitlyn for herself, but she didn't dare. As Immy looked up at the tree, she wondered if there was still a danger of Caitlyn being taken. It didn't make sense. It was *her* birthday coming up, not Caitlyn's. Immy knew that it was herself she should be worried about, but the truth was, as time passed, she was becoming worried about the tree in a different way entirely. The tree really didn't look well now. It seemed smaller somehow. As if it were trying to curl up inside itself and die. As she thought about this, something caught her eye. Something at the top of the tree, near her window . . .

Something brilliant and glittery hovering in one of its sagging branches.

She blinked and looked again. Was it the sun playing tricks on her eyes? No, something was definitely there. Something amethyst-colored and shimmering.

And then, just like that, it was gone.

Immy stood, almost knocking her water over in the process. "Did you see something? Up there. In the tree."

Erin looked up. "No. What was it?"

Immy's eyes searched for it again. "Something purple and bright."

Erin took another look at the barren tree. "Well, I don't think it was berries you saw. . . . Did you know there's a sort of story about this tree's berries? People say the tree used to have loads of fruit. Just like the one on the village green. That the whole village would stop by and pick some and take it home and make jam and pies and all sorts of things. But that was centuries ago. You know, before the first girl disappeared."

"The real estate woman said the same thing," Immy replied.

Both the girls stared upward, where not a leaf or bud was in sight. Both their expressions were doubtful.

"Do you think it's dying?" Erin said.

"I hope not," Immy replied quickly. She meant it, too.

"Maybe it was a bird you saw?" Erin said as Immy sat down again.

"Maybe," she replied slowly, trying to picture what she'd seen in her mind—a glint of bright, reddish-blue.

What if it wasn't a bird but something else? Like Jean had said, maybe it wasn't a person Elizabeth had seen outside her window. Not a person, or an animal, but something . . .

Magical.

Immy ducked in and out of the house all evening, trying to catch another glimpse of what she'd seen in the tree that afternoon.

She didn't see a thing.

"What on earth are you doing?" her mum said when she'd run outside and back in again for what felt like the five hundredth time during a commercial break on TV.

"Oh, just checking . . ."

"For what?"

"I . . . thought it might rain."

Immy sat back down on the sofa, her spine ramrod straight. Should she tell her parents what Jean had told her? Should she tell them she'd seen something? She felt like she shouldn't. It was strange, but she knew she was on the brink of something with the tree. An understanding. Could she trust the tree? Maybe it was trying to trick her into trusting it? Maybe that's what had happened to the other girls.

She really wasn't sure what to do or think.

They went upstairs to get ready for bed not long after that, and between having a shower and brushing her teeth, Immy peeked out of her bedroom window another five hundred times or so.

Still nothing.

After her dad had fed the hoglets, her parents both came in to say good night. Immy tried to sleep and couldn't, so she turned on her bedside lamp and read for a while, her eyes shifting to the open bedroom window every so often.

When she finally flicked the light off, she still couldn't sleep. Eventually she got up and brought her desk chair back to the window, where she sat and stared and waited and wondered.

Immy awoke to a noise, and her clouded mind attempted to remember something. She thought back and was surprised to find herself in her bed. She'd been sitting in her chair by the window, hadn't she? She couldn't recall crawling back into bed, but she must have.

Tap, tap.

The noise came again.

Tap, tap, tap.

It was coming from the open window.

She pushed back the covers and got up from her bed.

She approached the window cautiously, not knowing what to expect. What she might see.

What the tree wanted.

Because it was the tree tapping upon her window. Not the wind making the branches brush against the glass, but the actual tree. She knew it was.

It wasn't until she was standing right up against the window itself that she finally saw it properly — what she'd caught a glimpse of earlier that afternoon.

It was a berry—a single berry glinting and gleaming on one of the tree's slender branches.

With a cool breeze blowing in from outside, Immy stared at it, hypnotized.

She'd known, that afternoon. Known it hadn't been a bird she'd seen. Or something ordinary.

And it wasn't.

Because this berry was no ordinary berry. It was ablaze in the moonlight as if made of crystal, its colors changing from dark red to magenta to mauve and everything in between. It was the most beautiful thing she'd ever seen. It begged her to reach out and touch it. To take it. To taste it.

She'd never wanted to eat anything so much.

Without hesitating to consider the danger, Immy stretched out her hand.

And then she plucked the mulberry from the branch and ate it.

31

Elizabeth

Immy stood in the dark, next to the open window of her bedroom. To her right a shuffling noise made her jump. She whirled around to see what it was and, with a gasp, took a step back, clutching on to the windowsill as she realized there was someone in her bed. Except . . .

It wasn't her bed.

She looked around quickly in the half-light.

It wasn't her bed, and it wasn't her room. That is, it *was* her room, but it was different.

There was no desk or chair or lamp, and instead of the large wardrobe with the sliding glass door, there was a small, plain, wooden one.

Immy held her breath as she took one step closer to the bed. Long dark hair lay on the pillow.

Tap, tap, tap.

Immy's eyes moved back to the window. It was exactly the same noise she'd heard just moments ago—the noise that had wakened her. It seemed to be waking the girl in the bed now as well, because she turned in her sleep, disturbed.

Tap, tap, tap.

The girl shifted again, rolling over, and then, finally, sat up. She glanced around the room, seeking out the noise. Immy sucked in her breath as the girl saw her.

Until she realized the girl couldn't see her at all.

Instead of crying out or demanding to know who Immy was, the girl skimmed over Immy and took in the rest of the room.

Tap, tap, tap.

The insistent noise came again, making both sets of eyes snap toward the open window. Now the girl got out of bed and went over to peer out, just as Immy had done when the noise had woken her before.

Following her over there, Immy caught a glimpse

of the girl's features as she went, the moonlight shining in from outside.

The first thing she noticed was the girl's eyes.

Jean had spoken about someone with startling bright green eyes. Someone who had also lived in this room. Immy took in the furniture again.

The girl she was looking at could only be Elizabeth.

Her mouth hanging open in horror, Immy followed Elizabeth's gaze outside, already half knowing what she'd see.

And there it was.

A berry. The exact same sort of magical sparkling berry that she'd eaten herself.

Elizabeth stared at the berry, looking as mesmerized as Immy had felt. Immy, however, stared at something else. The tree—it was different. It didn't look like the tree she knew. Not only was there just one knot upon its trunk, but it was also darker. Fiercer. More menacing. The tree Immy knew was scary, but this tree—it was a tree of nightmares. When it had offered the berry to Immy, it had been asking her to take it. This was different. Now it dangled the berry in a different way. In a torturous way. As if it knew full well Elizabeth wouldn't be able to resist and was laughing at her feebleness to do so.

"Elizabeth!" Immy cried out, trying to grab her. "No! Don't . . ." Her hand passed straight through her.

It was too late anyway. Elizabeth had already taken the berry from the tree, and it was in her mouth.

Then, in the blink of an eye, she was gone.

As Immy looked around, the room began to steadily lighten. It took Immy a moment or two to realize what was happening—the day was moving forward quickly, as if someone had pressed fast-forward on a recording.

"Tree! What's happening?" Immy asked.

But she received no answer.

She watched as people entered and exited the room several times in a blur until, suddenly, the dizzy feeling that had come over her as her eyes struggled to keep up stopped. Now a man and a woman entered the room at a normal pace. Immy guessed they were Elizabeth's aunt and uncle—the people Jean had told her Elizabeth had lived with. They were older. Gray streaks ran through the woman's hair, which was pulled back in a bun, and the man was balding on top.

"I don't understand it." The woman moved over to the bed and smoothed the bedclothes. "Where could she have gotten to? I've checked with Jean's family. She hasn't been there at all. It simply doesn't make any sense."

Immy noted the woman looked more annoyed than worried.

"Ah, she'll turn up. I keep telling you," the man said. He turned and left the room with a shrug. "She's probably outside somewhere. Running up and down the street in her nightgown," he called back over his shoulder. "She's excited, is all."

After a moment or two, the woman followed him out. Immy decided to leave the room as well. She could see that the front door was open at the bottom of the stairs, and, as she made her way down, she could hear bells starting to peal from what must have been the village church down the road.

The man and the woman turned right, veering toward the kitchen, but Immy—hearing other voices—walked straight out the front door.

And then she stood stock-still as she attempted to take in the scene before her.

The usually quiet street had been closed down

and turned into a sea of red, white, and blue — the colors of the Union Jack on the British flag, which was prominently displayed everywhere. Flags rippled in the breeze; large and small, they hung from windows, were stuck into gates and hedges, and fluttered on bunting. All along the middle of the street were tables, each sporting a different tablecloth and set with different crockery. And everywhere — everywhere — were people. People laughing, people shouting, people dancing. There were men in uniform or trousers and shirts with the sleeves rolled up, and women in uniform or wool skirts and fancy blouses, their hair set in perfect waves atop their heads, scarlet lipstick on their lips. There were girls with tight braids and summer dresses, and boys in funny shorts, long socks, and buttoned shirts with vests over the top. Everyone from young to old wore paper party hats.

Immy couldn't believe her eyes as she looked around. She'd always thought that many people in this village seemed miserable. But these people were anything *but* miserable. A conga line danced around at one end of the table, another group was singing, and a couple of older men sat at a table with handkerchiefs on their heads to keep the sun off. She even saw one man dancing with a little dog.

It was then that she remembered the photograph she'd seen on the wall at the library. This was VE Day — the day of the biggest party Great Britain had ever seen, or probably would see. The war was over. She remembered something else, too. It was Elizabeth's birthday. Jean had told her so. Elizabeth had disappeared on VE Day, which also happened to be her eleventh birthday.

The people suddenly began to blur, and Immy realized time was moving on once more, in a swirl of red, white, and blue.

When the scene slowed for a second time, the shadows were starting to lengthen. Immy guessed it was midafternoon.

A booming voice came from a loudspeaker that had been set up in someone's front window. It sounded like a speech was being broadcast. It was obviously an important one that they'd been waiting to hear — maybe by the prime minister — but as she looked around, Immy began to notice that people weren't really listening. Instead, they were standing in small groups and talking. And looking worried.

Not far from Lavender Cottage's front gate, the man and woman whom Immy had seen in Elizabeth's bedroom were talking to a policeman. A girl was there as well. Immy ran over so she could listen in to what they were all saying.

The woman definitely looked far more anxious than before. She was twisting her hands worriedly now as she spoke. "She's gone. Simply gone! Something's wrong, I know it is. All her things are there. Even her clothes. It's not right."

The policeman didn't look too concerned. "These evacuees often don't settle well, and VE Day will have stirred everything up. My guess is she's run back to London."

The man and woman glanced at each other as the girl looked on. "No. No, I don't think so," the woman answered. "We're not strangers. We're family. She was very happy here. She had her friends. Her school. And she wouldn't go to London in her nightgown, would she?"

"You've got a point there, love," her husband said.

"It's the excitement of the day. Lots of the children will be up to high jinks." The policeman smiled kindly. "She'll be back before dark or will telephone before then. You'll see."

As he spoke, the girl standing with them began to look angrier and angrier. It was on closer inspection that Immy realized it was someone she knew.

It was Jean. The girl was Jean.

As soon as the policeman had finished speaking, Jean spoke up. "You don't understand," she said to him, her voice insistent. "Elizabeth wouldn't just run off. She told me everything. Everything! She was excited about today. It's her birthday. I have a present for her, and there's to be a cake later and everything. She was looking forward to that."

"Yes," her aunt said. "We managed a cake, even with the rationing. We've been saving our sugar up for some time."

A group of several men approached. "We're going to send out a few groups walking along the river. Just to look."

"Oh, thank you. Thank you," Elizabeth's aunt told them, her hand coming to her chest. "That would ease my mind. All I can think about is what if she's fallen and broken her leg? Or something's toppled upon her and she's trapped? Anything could have happened. Anything! We've all been so distracted today."

"You stay here, love," her husband told her. "Hopefully it's just that time's gotten away from her and she'll simply come back."

As the men walked off, the scene began to blur once more, and day moved on into night. Immy found herself standing alone on the now quiet street, the tables gone, the party packed up. Small groups of people still milled about, however, talking, whispering.

It was obvious that Elizabeth hadn't turned up.

And then a bloodcurdling scream cut through the quiet of the night.

Everyone ran in the direction of it, heading straight for the back garden of Lavender Cottage.

Immy, who had been standing just outside the house itself, was the first to reach the scene.

The first to see where the scream had come from.

It had come from Jean.

Jean, who stood, terrified, her hands splayed upon the brand-new knot on the mulberry tree.

"It's happened," she cried. "It's happened again."

3^2
Happy Birthday

Immy jolted awake, her whole body stiffening. She took a ragged breath.

A dream. It had all been a dream.

In the moonlight that shone through the window, she brought her hands to her sweaty face.

And froze when she saw the fingers on her right hand.

They were stained a deep blue-red.

She couldn't take her eyes off them and stared at her fingers for what felt like forever, trying to process what she'd seen. What she now knew.

Immy threw back her covers and flew from the bed. She ran to the open window, furious with the tree.

"You took her!" she hissed at the tree, wanting to scream but not wanting to wake her parents. "You really did it. That's what Elizabeth saw. What she told Jean about. It wasn't a person, or an animal. It was you all along. You *took* her! How could you? How could you do that? Where is she? Where have you put her?"

The tree drooped further, as if ashamed of itself.

"And what about Bridget? I bet you did exactly the same thing to her, didn't you? Show me! Show me what you did!"

The tree was all silence.

Immy braced herself, ready to ask her next question.

"And me! What have you got planned for me?"

She waited.

But no more explanation came.

Exhausted, Immy finally managed to get to sleep in the early hours of the morning, despite her feverish brain. She jolted awake once more when her mother called out her name.

"Immy, come *on*! This is the fifth time I've called

you! It's Friday. It's not the weekend yet!" her mum yelled up the stairs.

She threw her school uniform on, washed her face, and headed down to the kitchen. Her eyes felt dry and scratchy and her heart was heavy as she thought about what had happened last night. She couldn't stop looking at her fingers, which were still stained despite the vigorous scrubbing she'd just given them in the bathroom.

She found her parents both standing by the open French doors, staring outside at the tree.

"What is it?" she said quickly, running over to them.

Her dad glanced at her before turning back to the tree. "There really is something wrong with the tree," he said.

Immy pushed past them in order to get a better look. She was surprised to see that the tree looked even worse than it had last night. It truly did seem to be wilting now. Weakening. Dying.

"Well, we can't say anything about it now." Immy's mum shrugged. "Not after all that fuss from the owners. We'll wait until Monday. After the party."

"I think we can wait," Immy's dad said. "It's

sturdy enough. It's not going to fall on the house or anything."

Immy kept staring at the tree, hoping it could hear her every thought. To think she'd given it the benefit of the doubt. That she didn't believe it had taken Elizabeth and probably Bridget, too. And it had! She narrowed her eyes as she looked at it, wanting it to know she wouldn't let it take anyone else ever again.

She wouldn't be the third girl, and she'd make sure no one else ever became the third girl either.

At school that day, there was still no Caitlyn. Immy decided she'd ask Erin where Caitlyn lived. She kept thinking about those strange changes in Caitlyn. What if the tree was doing something to her? Getting ready to steal her away even though she wasn't living in Lavender Cottage? She had to see for herself what was going on with Caitlyn. Would she look different again? Maybe she'd had dreams, too?

But Erin arrived at school with news: Caitlyn's parents had taken her away. They thought she was stressed about the tree. About Immy's party. They'd gone to Norfolk for the weekend. Caitlyn wouldn't be back at school until next week.

During her lessons, Immy couldn't pay attention. All she could do was go over and over again in her head what she'd seen last night. She tried desperately to make sense of it all, but she simply couldn't. Elizabeth had disappeared when she ate the berry. Is that what had happened to Bridget, too? So why hadn't it happened to her as well? Why had the tree allowed her to come back? Why did the tree look so sick? Should she tell Jean what had happened? Her parents? The more she thought about it all, the more questions swirled around in her mind. They seemed to gather speed as they went, creating a confusing whirlwind.

Immy managed to struggle through the day and even went to allotment club in the afternoon. She hadn't planned on going, but when she got home, she saw the tree and decided she needed to get out of the house.

It was Mrs. Garland who noticed something was up. Immy had paused in between picking runner beans, and Mrs. Garland came over to squat down beside her. "Everything okay?" she asked her. "You seem a bit distracted today."

"Everything's fine," Immy said quickly. "Just, you know . . . thinking about the party."

Mrs. Garland nodded knowingly. "Don't you worry. I'm sure you'll have a good turnout and the village will be able to put all this behind us."

Immy doubted it but smiled and nodded and began picking runner beans once more.

She went through the front door when she got home again, not wanting to make her way around the back of the house near the tree. She couldn't bear to look at it. To be near it. She busied herself inside instead, feeding Cloud, Marshmallow, and Scramble and cleaning out their cage. That evening, in her bedroom, she kept the window closed and locked, despite the fact that it was a warm night.

She could barely sleep, wondering if the tree would wake her again. If it would try to take her. If she'd be able to resist the berry.

She needn't have been worried, because nothing happened.

No rhyme entered her head, and there was no eerie scratching at the window. No dream.

If anything, the tree was *too* silent as it waited. Waited and watched.

On Saturday morning, Immy's mum went to do her rounds at the hospital. Immy and her father fed the hoglets and then got ready to go grocery shopping. They had a long list of everything they needed to buy for the party.

As they approached the gardening section in front of the huge grocery store, Immy's dad paused, looking thoughtful.

"Let's just duck in for a minute," he said.

They ended up buying a pot of some sort of strange stuff her dad said was like food for the tree. "I've never seen a tree look so sorry for itself," he said as they waited to pay. "It honestly looks like something's eating it up from the inside."

"Maybe something is," Immy said, thinking of the two knots and Bridget and Elizabeth.

They began their grocery shopping after this. It wasn't until they'd put everything into their cart and were lining up at the checkout that it finally came to

Immy. She was putting a gigantic bottle of lemonade onto the conveyer belt when her eye caught a display of gift cards that read HAPPY BIRTHDAY. She almost dropped the lemonade on the floor but managed to catch it just in time.

Happy birthday.

Her birthday.

That's why the tree's berry hadn't taken her the other night. The tree had taken Bridget and Elizabeth on the *eve* of their birthdays.

The tree hadn't spared her at all.

It had shown her what was coming.

33

Out the Window

Immy's mind flip-flopped all afternoon as to what she should do. Should she tell Jean what she'd seen? Should she tell her parents? Should they go away like Caitlyn's family had done? Maybe back to the hotel they'd stayed at in Cambridge? She knew if she asked her parents if they could go there, they'd do it.

But she didn't want to ask.

Something inside her wanted to get to the bottom of this. To see if the tree would show her more. Now more than ever she wanted to find out why it had done what it had done. What if she could help Elizabeth in some way? Maybe Bridget, too? And then there was the strange change she'd seen in Caitlyn's behavior. In her eyes.

She had to keep going, and she knew if she told the adults around her what had happened, she'd simply be stopped.

Late in the day, Immy was sitting by the window in her room when she caught a glimpse of something moving in the back garden. She looked down to see Jean placing her white rose in the knot of the tree—the knot that had appeared when Elizabeth disappeared. When she was done, she glanced up at Immy's room, as if hoping to see her. Immy waved and gestured to say she was coming down. She knew that her parents were both reading in the living room, so she walked down the stairs at a normal pace, as if heading for the kitchen. When she was out of view, she raced across the dining room and was out the French doors in a flash.

"Ah," Jean said, taking one of her hands when Immy got to her. "I was hoping to catch you." She glanced up at the tree once more. "What do you make of this? There's something terribly wrong with the tree, isn't there?"

Immy nodded, visions of what she had seen bubbling up inside her. She pushed them back down.

She had to do this on her own. "Dad bought some special food for it, but I don't think it's done much good."

Jean nodded. "It's strange timing."

"Yes."

Jean's gaze moved back down to meet Immy's. She paused for a moment. "I just wanted to tell you I'm very much looking forward to your party tomorrow. . . ." She trailed off.

"And you're worried about tonight," Immy added for her.

"Well, I'd be lying if I said I wasn't. I certainly don't think I'll be getting much sleep." She looked up into the branches of the tree. "I can't stop thinking about Elizabeth. I keep wondering what she might have become. What she would have looked like. Where she would have lived. Who she might have married. About her children and grandchildren."

Immy couldn't think of anything to say.

Jean sighed. "Maybe . . . maybe she has those things. Somewhere. Somehow. I hope she does. I hope she's happy." Her hand that held Immy's trembled. "Goodness, but this has all brought everything back up again. . . ."

"Sorry," Immy said, remembering what she'd seen—the terror on the young Jean's face as she'd touched the newly formed knot in the tree. The horror as she realized she'd lost her friend.

"Oh, no." Jean shook her head. "Don't be sorry. It's been so refreshing to have you here. And I think a lovely party on your eleventh birthday is just what we need to start anew. To put this behind us once and for all."

Immy gulped and gave her a small nod. Jean was right. A party on her eleventh birthday would be perfect. At least, it would be as long as she didn't disappear the night before.

"Well, this is it," Immy's dad said that evening as she lay reading in bed. He crossed her room, closed the window and locked it, and shut the curtains tight.

"Sure you don't want to sleep in our room?" her mum asked, leaning against the door frame. "We could set up your mattress on the floor."

Immy tried to remain calm, despite the crazy beating of her heart. "Don't be silly," she said. "It's like we said when we moved in—trees can't steal people. I'll be fine." If her voice sounded shaky, her parents didn't seem to notice.

"All right, then," her mother said. "Don't read too long, will you? We've got a big day tomorrow."

"I won't."

Her dad hovered over her bed. "We've checked and double-checked—all the doors and windows are locked. We're safe and sound. So, off to sleep, and don't let the bedbugs, or the nasty tree, bite." He leaned over and gave her a kiss on her forehead. "Good night, sweetheart. Love you."

"Love you, too," Immy said, her heart truly racing now. What was going to happen this evening? Might this be the last time she would ever see her parents? "Both of you," she added quickly, scared it might really be true.

Her mother crossed the room and gave her a kiss as well. "Good night, lovely girl."

Immy had to turn her head as they left the room, scared she'd let the tears that were welling up behind her eyes spill over.

* * *

Tap, tap.

Tap, tap, tap.

Having been drifting in and out of sleep since switching the lights off, Immy took only seconds to sit up, wide awake.

She gasped when she saw the curtains billowing and the window pushed open despite the fact that her dad had closed it and locked it carefully.

Throwing off her sheet and blanket, she went over to the window, her eyes drawn to the tree outside.

The tree she'd seen this afternoon had struggled to hold up its own branches. And now it seemed weaker still, as if it were channeling the very last of its will into what it held out to her now . . .

Another deep-red, ripe, shimmering mulberry.

Take me. It sparkled and shone in the moonlight. *Take me and eat me. You know you want to. You know you have to.*

There was no resisting it.

She had to take it.

And so she did.

Immy's fingers reached out and plucked the mulberry from the tree, then put the radiant fruit in her mouth.

In the blink of an eye, the room whirled around her and she found herself standing in the very same room in the middle of a bright, sunny day. However, it was a different room again. It wasn't hers or Elizabeth's. This room was plain white, though it was still crisscrossed with the heavy, dark beams. There were even fewer items within it than had been in Elizabeth's room. Now there were only a heavy wooden bed that seemed impossibly small—a thin mattress on it and a rough woolen blanket spread on top of linen sheets—a chest of drawers, and a matching wooden washstand with a pretty bowl and jug on top.

Not hearing or seeing any people, Immy turned back to the window.

Her eyes widened in disbelief.

Because there was the tree.

And here, in this time, it was a different tree altogether.

34

A Different Tree

It wasn't that the mulberry tree was smaller and younger that had surprised Immy but something else entirely. It was as Erin and Helen, the real estate agent, had said—once upon a time, the tree had berries. And not just a little but a lot. This version of the tree was leafy and green and absolutely groaning with fruit. So much so, its branches drooped for an entirely different reason than they did in Immy's time. Every single branch was laden with plump mulberries ranging from crimson to deep, dark vermillion and all the colors in between. Just by looking at them Immy could tell they would be sweet and delicious and perfect for making pies and jams and cordials. It reminded her of the tree on the village green, just bigger and even better at growing its fruit.

Unlike the tree Immy knew from Lavender Cottage's back garden, this version of the tree gave off a happy, contented feeling. Its green leaves fluttered in the breeze, and there was no lean to it. Instead, it stood tall and proud next to the house. It looked like a tree that was quite sure it was loved by the village, which it provided sweet treats for.

Thinking of the village and its inhabitants, Immy's gaze moved down the trunk of the tree. There were no knots to be seen at all.

Her attention moved to the rest of the garden, which was also different in this time period. For a start, there was another tree in the garden. A smaller, far younger mulberry. It was also leafy and green, but it bore no fruit, unlike its far larger friend. Immy remembered the dip in the grass that they had to be careful of in their time. It was in exactly the same spot. It must have been where the tree had been removed at some point like her dad thought might have happened.

To the right of the smaller tree was a strange

sort of clothesline — not like anything people had today. This clothesline was very long and seemed to be propped up with wooden poles. A sheet upon it flapped in the breeze, held on by wooden pegs. Every so often, the sheet flapped against the smaller tree.

Immy's eyes on the sheet, she realized it was beginning to flap faster and faster. Time was moving forward again, just as it had done when she had visited Elizabeth's home.

Night turned to day and day turned to night and then day again as the tree prepared to show her important happenings from its past. Finally, time slowed once more. Now there were people in the garden. There was a woman in a long dark blue dress with a small pattern on it. Her hair was covered by a sort of bonnet with a sheer fabric on top of it, and the same fabric covered her shoulders and was tucked into the neckline of the dress. The woman stood with two men who were dressed in coarser clothes — brown trousers and grubby-looking shirts. They seemed to be workmen of some kind, because one had an ax and one had a shovel. Just as the woman was about to speak, a boy and a girl ran into the garden, chasing each other and screeching playfully. The girl held up the skirt of her long cream-colored cotton dress as she ran.

"Bridget!" the woman called out. "Do stop that noise at once."

Immy focused in on the girl quickly. It had to be her Bridget. She was fair, with distinctive strawberry blond hair, and she seemed sweet and playful, chasing her little brother, who had dark hair. He was loving every minute of the fun.

"Mama! Mama! Look at me!" The boy screeched this time as they rounded the larger tree.

"Bridget! Must I remind you that you will be eleven years of age tomorrow?" The woman sighed as she turned back to the men. "I do despair, I honestly do. Now, here, it's as I told you—that tree, the smaller one." She gestured toward it. "It hasn't had a great deal of fruit and it's only getting in the way of the laundry now."

"You don't want us to cut it down, missus?"

The woman shook her head. "The vicar has been most insistent that we should move it to the village green. He seems to think it might come into its own there. Being the offspring of the larger tree, it could provide as much fruit as its relative when it's older, though I'm not entirely convinced of this myself. He has agreed to pay for its removal, however, and thus I won't argue with him on that point."

The men glanced at each other, looking like they'd prefer to simply cut the tree down, but they dipped their hats, and it seemed they'd do as they were asked.

"Come now, children! Come inside. Leave the men to their business." The woman herded the boy and girl inside, and the men started toward the smaller tree.

Time moved on again then, and with a *whoosh*, light turned to darkness once more.

Must I remind you that you will be eleven years of age tomorrow? Immy recalled the woman's words as blurred stars appeared overhead.

Bridget's birthday was fast approaching.

Or maybe it was even closer than she thought. Because in the dark, as Immy turned from the window toward the bed, she realized that there was someone in the room with her.

It was Bridget, of course, her strawberry blond hair in a loose braid that hung over the side of the bed. She was sleeping, just as Elizabeth had been. Just as Immy had been until . . .

Tap. Tap, tap.

Tap, tap.

Bridget rolled over.

Tap, tap, tap. Tap, tap, tap.

The tapping became more insistent now.

Bridget sat up, stretching and yawning. She looked around.

Tap, tap, tap, tap, tap, tap, tap.

The tree wasn't going to take no for an answer.

Frowning, Bridget pushed back the woolen blanket and rose from her bed. She approached the window cautiously, pausing midway across the room. As she did so, Immy was able to see her properly in the moonlight that came in through the window. Her hair shone like spun gold, and Immy found herself trying to work out the relationship between strawberry blond Bridget and dark-haired, green-eyed Elizabeth. With Bridget gone, the house had probably been left to the boy she had seen Bridget with in the garden, Immy realized. And then it would have been passed on down from there, ending up with the man and woman who had cared for Elizabeth, their niece. And from there, it had gone to a nephew, who was Caitlyn's father. Immy bit her lip as she realized who Caitlyn looked like, with her dark hair and dark eyes—Bridget's brother.

Paying attention to her surroundings once more, Immy frowned as she looked at Bridget. What was wrong with her? She was still standing in the same spot in the middle of the room, staring out the window, but now she had a hand clamped over her mouth.

Immy whirled around to look out the window herself. She hadn't really taken in the view yet, preoccupied as she had been with Bridget.

She froze when her eyes finally caught what was outside.

It was the mulberry tree. It had completely transformed in the space of only a few hours. It had dropped all of its fruit and all of its leaves on the ground, which was now stained a dark red, almost like blood, the stain seeping into all four corners of the garden. It leaned threateningly over the house, just as it did in the present day.

The previously contented tree was now furious. Immy could feel its rage in the air like static electricity. Like a silent scream.

Only one bright note remained—the bewitching

berry. The very first one. It bobbed enticingly near Bridget's window, absolutely dazzling and even more tempting than the ones that had come after it. The mulberry tree wanted Bridget to eat that mulberry very badly indeed and couldn't wait for her to do so.

Bridget blinked, staring at the strange, unfamiliar sight. And then, slowly, her fingers reached out.

"No!" Immy screamed at her, stepping forward to try to stop her. But her hands only moved straight through Bridget's body, just as they'd done with Elizabeth's. "Don't eat it, Bridget!" she called out, knowing her cries were useless. "Don't do it!"

Seconds later, Bridget was gone.

Immy leaned out the window and looked down, her hand upon her heart, knowing what she would see.

There, stark in the moonlight, it was—the very first knot upon the tree.

35

. . . One, Two, Three

Immy expected to be returned to her room.

But that wasn't what happened.

Instead, her surroundings whirled around her once more. She had to grip on to the windowsill as she started to feel dizzy and light in the head.

When the world had righted itself again, Immy was surprised to find herself looking at Bridget's bed and not her own. But it took only seconds before the commotion outside registered, and still gripping on to the windowsill, she swiveled to take in the tree, outside.

The tree was still there, dark and enraged and brimming with hate. It was raining heavily outside, the sky sooty and gray. The wind whipped around the garden, leaves flying through the air, the tree's branches swishing violently this way and that.

Through this madness came a single man. Drenched almost as soon as he left the house, he dragged a large ax with him.

As he passed under the tree, one of its branches swooped down and caught him with a hard *thwack*, but he continued on as if he'd barely even noticed and made his way directly to its trunk.

He must have known he wouldn't be able to cut the tree down by himself, but he didn't seem to care. He simply took up his position and lashed out at the thick, gnarled, blackened bark in front of him. Over and over again he pounded the tree with the ax. Over and over and over, like a thing possessed.

The marks on the tree, Immy remembered. The marks she and her father had seen. That's how those marks had been made.

The man kept going, his hands red-raw and bleeding. It was heartbreaking to watch, because Immy knew the man could only be Bridget's father, devastated that his daughter was gone.

Finally, a woman ran out in the rain—Bridget's

mother. She was soon followed by Bridget's dark-haired younger brother, who grabbed at his mother's skirt, silent, his deep brown eyes wide and scared. The pair stood and watched the man for some time, becoming drenched themselves. Then he saw them. Falling to his knees, he dropped the ax. They ran over to him and huddled in a group in the mud.

The world started spinning again, and Immy had to close her eyes.

It took Immy a moment or two to realize she was back in her own room. There was the desk. The chair. The iron bed frame. The glass of the large built-in wardrobe.

Continuing to grip the windowsill, she looked out at the fading tree outside.

"You took those two girls," she said to the tree. "How could you? How could you do that? What did you do with them? Where did they go?"

No reply came.

Immy shook her head. "I can't believe I trusted you. I defended you. And it was you all along. You are evil! You are!" As she stared at the tree in disbelief, she remembered what Jean had said to her — about how the tree had taken all of Elizabeth's birthdays. It had taken the children she would never have. Her grandchildren. Her happiness. Jean had hoped that somewhere, somehow, Elizabeth was still alive. That she had those things. That she was happy.

But she wasn't.

Elizabeth didn't have those things. She wasn't happy. And neither was Bridget. It was all the tree's fault. This terrible, awful, sickly tree in front of her. It had secreted those girls somewhere. Some place deep inside itself. Hidden them. Hoarded them.

Immy's fingernails dug hard into the wood of the windowsill. There was so much hate that Immy wanted to spew at the tree. Caught in a whirlwind of feelings, she tried to form sentences and failed, tired and overwhelmed by what she had seen. In the end, she could manage to come up with only one word.

"Why?" she asked the tree. *"Why?"*

Immy wasn't sure she even expected an answer. But then she held her breath as the tree began, slowly, to move.

It creaked and groaned and inched its way

forward, as if it hurt to do so, its branches bending back from the house to move over to the place where the smaller tree had once stood. It hugged the spot protectively like the smaller tree was still there. Or as if it wished it were.

"What? Because they took your friend away?" Immy frowned. She didn't understand. "That's it? That's all?"

The tree only embraced the empty spot harder.

Immy shook her head as she watched. Something about the action reminded her of Bridget's family embracing, and her forehead creased. Thinking back, Immy recalled something Bridget's mother had said when Immy had first seen her in the garden. Something about the smaller tree . . .

She cried out, finally understanding. Finally seeing.

"They took your *daughter*." Immy's hand came to her chest.

The tree made a movement that looked decidedly like a nod.

"The smaller tree — it was your daughter, and they took her away on the eve of Bridget's eleventh birthday. And so . . . so you took theirs. First Bridget. Then Elizabeth and . . ." She paused, closing her eyes, as the sickening rhyme came back to her, beginning to play out in her head once more:

Do naught wrong by the mulberry tree,
or she'll take your daughters . . .

one,

two,

three.

In the dead of night, spirited away,
never to see an eleventh birthday.

"An eye for an eye . . . and a daughter for a daughter," Immy finally said, her eyelids flickering open once more. "Oh, tree," she said, sighing. "Oh, tree." The tears began rolling down her cheeks as she realized the awfulness of it all. She stretched out her hand and took one of the tree's branches without hesitation, its rough bark displaying all too well its feeling of despair.

Eventually the tree pulled away, its branches moving creakily back to their earlier position, though it now seemed even more hunched over than before. Immy could see that it didn't have long to live. It really was going to let itself wither and die.

She cried even harder then. For Bridget. For Elizabeth. For their families. For the tree.

So much pain.

So much hurt.

Immy's head fell into her hands. There had been too much pain and hurt in her life lately because of what had happened that led to their moving here. Immy wasn't sure how much more of it she could bear. And the tree—it had been in pain, too. It had been in pain for so very long. Immy felt terrible. She'd been so ready to hate the tree, just like everyone else in the village. Well, maybe not everyone. . . . She remembered Mrs. Garland telling her that there was no such thing as something being purely good or purely evil. And now that she'd witnessed the tree's side of the story, she knew Mrs. Garland was right. Angry about having its daughter stripped from its presence, the tree had simply lashed out. It had taken it centuries to realize it had been wrong in what it had done.

The choices the tree had made reminded Immy of somebody else's choices, too—Bob's. Bob, who had also lashed out impulsively and taken matters into his own hands and robbed a mother and daughter of their futures, just like Bridget and Elizabeth had been robbed of theirs.

Finally Immy understood.

She hadn't been able to understand it at the time, but now it was clear to her why her father had been kind to Bob. She remembered how he'd told her Bob had built his own prison. The tree had done that, too, in a way. It was the wronged party, but it had imprisoned itself in its own hate.

In that moment, Immy understood so well how powerless her father had been feeling lately. Because she was powerless in this moment, too. Now she knew the truth, but there was nothing she could do to make things better. For Bridget. For Elizabeth. For the tree.

For any of them.

36

A Plan

Immy drew her desk chair close to the window and sat on it, her knees hugged in to her chest. She watched the tree sicken and dim by the hour, feeling utterly powerless.

She couldn't give those girls their lives back.

She couldn't help the tree.

Immy sat and stared wistfully over toward the village green for a long time. She thought about the tree and its long life, which seemed to be coming to an end. Perhaps it was simply the tree's time to go? Nothing could live forever, and it seemed old and tired compared to that other mulberry tree—the one on the village green itself—which was so alive and full of fruit. And that was when all the pieces of the puzzle came together for her.

Her knees dropped and she sat up in her seat.

Of course!

No, she couldn't change the past and she couldn't give those girls their lives back, but there *was* one small thing she could do. One act of kindness. And maybe that's how things could start to get better. How everyone could start to heal.

Immy got up and padded silently across the room and out into the hallway, from where she made her way downstairs, skipping over every squeak she knew the house was capable of making.

In the living room, she could hear the hedge-hogs rustling about in their special cage. But there was no time to stop and greet them. Immy tiptoed into the dining room, went over to the cupboard, and grabbed her dad's phone. Then she sat down at the table and searched for something. It didn't take long to find exactly what she was looking for, and when she had the information she needed, she replaced the phone. Thinking for a moment, she decided not to go out the French doors in case her parents heard her. Instead, she crept out the front door, leaving it unlocked behind her.

Immy rounded the corner of the house and stayed close to the hedge. She paused about halfway to the shed and glanced up at her parents' room. The lights remained off. They hadn't heard her leave the house. She swiveled to look at what she could see of Jean's house, which was also still and dark.

So far, so good.

Quickly and quietly, she ran over and opened the shed door with only the smallest of squeaks from the hinges. It wasn't difficult to find what she needed. The shed was almost empty save for the few gardening bits and pieces that had been left behind, and there was a little glass window that the moon shone through. Immy spied what she'd come for, and she picked the pruning shears with their long wooden handles up off the table and left the shed once more.

She ran to the side gate, which led to the village green, being careful to stick to the shadows.

All was peaceful in the still of the night.

By the light of the moon, Immy pulled up the latch that held the gate shut and silently closed it behind her again.

It was only a short run over to the tree on the

green. She stopped before she reached it and stared up at it, just like she'd done the first time she saw it, though she hadn't known then what it was.

Who it was.

The daughter tree was much, much larger than the tree that had been in Bridget's back garden, though nothing compared with its mother.

It didn't remember, of course. It had been young when it was taken. And because of this, it had embraced its new life. Grown. Flourished. Shared its fruit generously with the village, just as its mother used to do long ago. Immy took the last few steps to reach out and stroke the tree's trunk.

"Hello," she said, the bark rough under her palm. "I don't know if you remember, but you used to live somewhere else. And I don't want to hurt you, but the thing is, I need to give you a little snip. Is that all right?"

The tree remained very, very still, as if considering Immy's offer.

"The thing is"—she looked up at the tree, right up to the very top branches, almost expecting to see a face—"I'm going to take you home. Home to your mother."

* * *

Immy took a large clipping with the pruning shears, apologizing to the tree as she did so. Then she ran home again, rounding the corner of the cottage in a heartbeat, excited to show the mulberry tree what she had in her hands.

But when she rounded the corner, she saw that the mulberry tree had declined even further, weary with its lot. There was no time to lose. Immy ran over to it.

"Look, tree, look! I have something for you!" she held up what was in her hands. "Watch! Watch me!" She went over to pat the ground with her feet until she found the dip in the grass.

There it was.

She got down on her hands and knees and made a small hole with the shears. She began to dig out a little earth with the handle. According to what she'd looked up on the internet, it would be simple. All she needed to do was . . .

"There!" She stuck the cutting into the ground and then shaped the displaced earth back around it.

As she did so, she had another idea. Scrambling to her feet, she ran across the garden, stumbling in her haste, and pulled the hedgehogs' playpen back with her. When it was close, she lifted one end so that the cutting was safely under it and then dragged the playpen a little farther, until the cutting was in the middle. Then she put the shears back in the shed and brought the watering can back with her. It still had some water in it, and she watered the cutting with this.

It was only when she focused back in on the larger tree that she saw it had pulled itself into more of an upright position. "Come on, come and look!" Immy grinned, beckoning it over. As she watched, two of its largest branches slowly stretched over — unsure, uncertain. As it rustled above her, Immy stared in wonder. Was she still dreaming? She honestly didn't know.

The tree bent down closer, as if inspecting the cutting. And then, slowly but surely, one thin, blackened finger reached out and touched it.

The moment the tree made contact, it startled, all of its branches standing to attention, suddenly very alive indeed. It was as if the tree had woken up inside itself. As if it had been given a new lease on life. A reason to live.

Immy smiled as she looked on. One thing she was certain of: if she was still dreaming, it was by far the best dream she'd ever had.

37
New Friends

"Happy birthday, sleepyhead." Immy's dad sat down on the edge of her bed. "Time to get up. It's eight thirty!"

Immy's eyes opened a crack. Light streamed into the room from the open window. It was morning. It was the morning of her eleventh birthday. She opened her eyes wide.

"Hey, I'm still here!" she said to her dad as she pushed herself up onto her elbows.

He gave her a funny look. "Where else would you be?"

Immy frowned. "You know, gone."

"Gone where?"

She blinked. "As in, disappeared."

He laughed, got up, and headed for the door. "I think you're still dreaming. Come on, come downstairs and open up your presents. Then we'd best start getting ready for the party."

"Okay." Immy swung her legs out of the bed and stood up, yawning and stretching.

As her dad thumped down the stairs, she crossed the room to see how the mulberry tree and its daughter were doing. She was hoping the older tree might look even healthier this morning. But when she got to the window, she was met with a completely unexpected sight.

"Oh!" Immy pushed the window open as far as it would go and leaned out.

The tree! The tree was like the tree of old — green and rich and full of fruit. But this wasn't all she saw. She checked once. Twice. And it was true — her eyes weren't playing tricks on her. "Oh, tree!" she cried out. "Tree! You're all better!"

She whirled about and, racing from the room, took the stairs two at a time.

She rounded the corner into the dining room and kept going, passing straight by her mother and father.

"Um, happy birthday!" her mother called out as she passed by and bolted out the French doors.

Immy ran straight to the tree, not stopping until both hands were on its thick trunk, moving up and down, feeling for what she hadn't been able to see from her room.

It really was true.

The knots.

The knots were gone.

Immy opened her presents and ate breakfast on autopilot, trying to work out exactly what was going on. The tree was healthy, the knots in its trunk had disappeared, and her dad hadn't seemed to know what she was talking about when she mentioned that she hadn't been taken in the night. Her parents had, however, been surprised to see the cutting with the hedgehogs' playpen around it.

"What's that about?" her mother asked.

"Oh, I thought the mulberry tree needed a friend," Immy said, buttering her toast. She remembered something she'd read on her dad's phone. "Apparently it's good for them to have other trees nearby. For the fruit or something."

Her dad snorted. "Well, I don't think the tree needs any help in the fruit department. More mulberry jam? We only have another twenty jars left to eat. We really should give some away today." He pushed a jar of jam across the table.

Immy stared at it in disbelief.

"Twenty jars? And they all came from the tree?"

"Have you honestly blacked out our jam-making weekend? I know it took us the whole two days, but it wasn't that awful, was it?"

"I, er . . ." They'd spent a whole weekend making jam? Out of mulberries from the tree?

"Yes, yes, it's amazing that we finally made something edible, I know. It's funny, but maybe I'm blacking things out, too. I hadn't even noticed you'd brought that cutting home and planted it."

"Mmm . . ." Immy said. She had a million other questions, but she couldn't help stuffing her mouth full of toast.

The jam was the best she'd ever tasted. Sweet and bursting with flavor.

After breakfast, they started to get ready for the party.

Everyone was going to arrive at ten thirty—all ten or so guests who had RSVP'd. But it was when a catering truck pulled up at the front of the house that Immy realized the guest numbers might have changed. The catering man and Immy's parents started to unload trays of finger sandwiches and miniature quiches and scones. Immy stood in the hallway and watched, agog.

"Um, how many people are coming?" she asked her dad, who was passing by with yet another tray of food.

"About fifty. You know that! We went through the list last night."

Immy's heart began to race. "Oh, um, yeah. Of course. I . . . forgot."

The day became stranger still as the guests began to arrive. Immy quickly worked out that there was no longer one single class of her year level at school but two. And there were *a lot* more girls. As she greeted them in the middle of the party's purple bunting and streamers, she had to pretend she knew them all, because they all seemed to know her.

Even stranger, quite a few of them had the same shade of strawberry blond hair.

Yet another one of these strawberry blond people came up to Immy now as she stood next to Riley. "Happy birthday, Immy!" the girl said. "This is for you." She passed her a present.

"Thanks, um . . . I mean, thanks so much!"

But the girl had already run off.

"Who was that?" Immy asked Riley.

Riley gave her a strange look. "Molly. She's in our class. And in the allotment club, remember?"

"Oh, yes, of course," Immy replied, as if she'd known this all along.

Riley was still looking at her. "You're really bad with names, aren't you?"

Immy nodded. *Especially with people I've never met before,* she thought. Riley still beside her, a thought crossed her mind. "Hey, remember the time we went to the library?" she said, testing out her theory.

"Which time? We go every week at school."

"No, the *other* library."

"What other library? I've only ever been to the school library with you."

Immy paused to think. So she'd been right. She put a blank look on her face. "Sorry, I was thinking about someone else. Come on, let's get something to drink." She dragged him off.

When Erin finally arrived, Immy was relieved to see another face she actually knew. She came over and gave Immy a hug.

"Happy birthday!" she said, handing her a wrapped present. "Oh!" She jumped out of the way as a mulberry fell from above, almost hitting her white dress. She laughed. "Smart move on the purple dress, Immy."

Immy looked down at her dress, which had been a birthday present from her parents. "Trust me, I didn't plan it," she told Erin. But had her parents? Maybe. Maybe they had, because she was starting to see what might have happened here.

"Hi!" Someone else ran over, a wide smile on her face, and presented her with a gift. "Happy birthday, Immy!"

For a moment, Immy thought it was some kind of joke. Zara? Zara was being nice to her?

She didn't have time to question Zara's actions for long, however, because Immy's mother came over, interrupting them.

"Immy," she said, "Jean's just come in. Would you mind making sure she finds a chair?"

"Sure," Immy said, leaving Zara and Erin chatting away happily together.

She glanced over to see Jean in the distance, making her way through the little wooden gate, along with another older woman whom she didn't know. A girl Immy didn't recognize followed close behind them.

"Hi, Jean," Immy said when she reached her.

"Happy birthday, Immy!" Jean said, handing her a small present. "What a lovely day for your party. Now, I hope it's all right, but I've brought a friend with me from the next village over, as she was visiting this morning."

"Sure," Immy said.

"This is Elizabeth."

Immy's head jerked back in surprise. She focused carefully on the woman standing before her. Of course. Of course it was Elizabeth. She might be much older, but those incredibly bright green eyes—they were exactly the same. Exactly! Immy should have known her the moment she'd seen her.

"Hello, Immy," Elizabeth said. "A happy birthday to you. You know my grandniece, Caitlyn, of course, from your class." Caitlyn was a living combination of Bridget and Elizabeth. Here their genes were, standing right in front of her.

Immy took a step back in fright as the girl, who had been busy closing the gate, approached her. As she took her in, she blinked. Blinked again.

Because the girl who was walking toward her was Caitlyn but not Caitlyn.

This girl had almost the same features as the Caitlyn she knew, but instead of deep brown eyes, she had the same vivid green as Elizabeth. Instead of dark hair, hers was the strawberry blond of Bridget's. Finally, Immy understood. With the return of the girls, their distinctive features had also reappeared in the village.

These weren't the only differences—the biggest change of all was the fact that instead of a scowl, Caitlyn wore a smile. Never having lived with the constant anger of the tree, she was a happier, sunnier person.

"Happy birthday, Immy!" Caitlyn said, grinning at her and passing her a huge, badly wrapped bundle. "You've got to open it now. Not just because it looks hideous but because I've been dying to give it to you. Go on!"

Immy couldn't stop staring at the change in her. What she'd noticed at school — those red highlights in her hair, the lightening of her eyes — were the tree's doing. It had been righting its wrongs. It had been changing the past. That's what had been draining it. Making it sick and tired.

She thought back over the past week or so. About how Caitlyn had whispered "I'm sorry" and Immy hadn't believed she could have heard her correctly. At the change in her hair. Her eyes. At how she'd sought out Immy in the school library but felt too sick to say anything. To explain.

It was just as Erin had said that day when she'd looked on.

It's almost like she's a different person.

She was.

"Immy! Come on!" Caitlyn urged her on.

It took everything inside Immy to be able to concentrate on the simple task of unwrapping the present, her fingers all feeling like thumbs.

It was a doormat, of all things. A doormat with a large picture of a hedgehog on it.

"I thought it looked just like Scramble!" Caitlyn said with a laugh.

All Immy could do was nod and smile.

"I'll be back in a minute, okay? I'm just going to go and say hello to Erin and Zara," Caitlyn told her, running off.

"And I'm going to have a short sit down on that seat right there," Jean said. "It's been a very busy morning."

Which left Elizabeth and Immy standing by themselves, contemplating the party.

And the tree.

The happy, fruit-filled tree, offering shade and protection to all below it.

Overwhelmed by what had happened, Immy stared around in disbelief, the doormat hanging limply in her hands.

The jam. The guest list. All the girls she'd never met before. The nonexistent trip to the library with Riley. It was honestly like it had all never happened. The tree had never taken those girls. It hadn't stolen Bridget or Elizabeth. It hadn't cast its dark anger over the village for hundreds of years. Because it hadn't done these things, the village was entirely different for it. There were girls at the school. Bridget and Elizabeth had lived long lives and had had families. Caitlyn was Elizabeth's grandniece, and she wasn't bitter or mean.

Immy looked around the garden. At Caitlyn's dad giving her dad tips on how to care for the hedges, at Zara's dad helping to pour drinks, at Riley talking to Jean and Mrs. Garland.

And, of course, at the tree, above.

There it stood, beautiful and green and alive. Below, beneath her feet, she felt its roots spread wide, offering strength and security and a sense of togetherness to everyone in the village. Immy stepped forward and stroked it. Only kindness and love radiated from its bark now.

You gave them back, Immy thought, hoping the tree could hear her. *That's what was making you sick. You gave them back without knowing you'd receive anything in return.*

Immediately, a wave of peace washed over Immy, almost as if the tree were sending her a message in return. Hoping to connect with it further, she kept her hand on the tree's trunk and closed her eyes.

It worked.

A word began to repeat over and over again in her head.

Forgiveness.

Immy opened her eyes again. A smile on her face, she tilted her head back and was met with a view of the tree's berried branches.

Forgiveness.

That was the tree's message.

By forgiving the village and freeing the girls, the tree had also freed itself.

Immy felt a hand on her shoulder. She looked up to see Elizabeth, who was taking in the tree's majesty as well.

It was some time before either of them spoke.

"Imagine being so old. The things it must have seen! I often think they must be very wise, trees," Elizabeth finally said.

"Yes," Immy replied, after a few strokes of the tree's beautiful knot-free trunk. "I think you're right. They are. Especially this one."

Acknowledgments

To all at Walker Books Australia, a bigger-than-the-mulberry-tree thank-you — Linsay Knight, Nicola Santilli, Sarah Ambrose, Amy Daoud, Anna Abignano, and everyone behind the scenes. Also to Rovina Cai for the beautiful cover illustration.

To my previous agent, Jaida Temperly, of New Leaf Literary & Media for the literal new leaf, and to Jordan Hamessley for taking over the reins.

As always, pats for my literate guinea pigs — Mum, Dad, Nilly, Paul, and David.

And to Allison Tait for the moral support and plotting of Zen and the Art of Publishing workshops.